N25 (7-91) 1

H 7-94

WITHDRAWN

MAMA'S DISAPPOINTMENT

MAMA'S DISAPPOINTMENT

Judy Christenberry

Walker and Company
New York

fic

First published in the United States of America in 1991 by
Walker Publishing Company, Inc.
Published simultaneously in Canada by Thomas Allen & Son
Canada, Limited, Markham, Ontario

Library of Congress Cataloging-in-Publication Data
Christenberry, Judy
Mama's Disappointment / Judy Christenberry
p. cm.
ISBN 0-8027-1163-4
I. Title.
PS3553.H69M36 1991
813'.54—dc20   90-25056
CIP

Printed in the United States of America
2   4   6   8   10   9   7   5   3   1

= 1 =

"EMMA, YOU ARE such a disappointment to me. Your step-sister was the belle of every ball, always fluttering around, dancing with all the most eligible men. Why you had to take after your father's side of the family I'll never know. Your mother was quite a beauty."

Mrs. Chadwell gave her overdressed hair a pat, knocking a large purple ostrich feather askew as she continued her monologue. "Your stepsister, of course, took after my family. We have always been quite a fetching lot. But you are so tall, so . . . so . . . Oh, it's no use even talking about it. But how you are going to attract a rich husband when you put not the least little effort into it, I'll never know."

Emma Chadwell stared straight ahead, as she had done for most of the evening, a vacant look on her face that discouraged any who might approach her.

This was not the first ball Emma and her stepmother had attended. They followed the same pattern at every entertainment. Mrs. Chadwell scolded her charge, talking without pause until the young woman's lack of response and the lure of the card tables distracted her from her role as chaperone.

Nearly always silent unless addressed, Emma remained expressionless and unappealing, never allowing a smile to cross her lips. At first, there were whispers and jokes made at her expense, but after a month of such behaviour, the young lady had come to be as much ignored as the numerous servants employed by the *ton*.

"Child, have you heard the least word I've said? If you don't marry someone with enough money to pay our debts, your beloved estate will have to be put on the market!"

There was a flash of fire in Miss Chadwell's large brown eyes, swiftly cloaked by her lowered lashes.

"I swear, I see no point in keeping it anyway," Mrs. Chadwell said. "It's far from London and life is so dull there."

"The reason for keeping it is the fact it is our main source of income, and it will continue to produce a profit if it is properly run," was the young woman's calm response.

"Don't tell me that. I saw that bill the squire sent you for his hay. Why, that amount alone could buy an entire wardrobe for me!"

Emma Chadwell smiled wryly. Her stepmother had not seen the bill of sale for the bulls she marketed early this spring, and she had no intention of informing her that the hay was well worth the investment. Even her brother, the owner of their estate, had no idea how much profit it made. He left everything in his sister's hands and used his time to find new and unique ways to lose his inheritance.

"Look, there is Lord Atherton and his friend, Mr. Fairchild. While the man has no title, he is twice as rich as Lord Atherton, but either would be a wonderful catch, my dear. Sit up and try to look more interested." When her stepdaughter's face grew more wooden than ever, she sighed. "You are such a disappointment to me, Emma."

Sure that the gentlemen were only passing by, reviewing the beauties to whom they would extend an invitation to dance, Emma turned her thoughts to her beloved home once more. She was long used to enduring the endless evenings upon which her stepmother insisted. By planning new techniques to be used on the estate, or the crops to be sown the next year, she was able to survive the torturous hours.

Even so, she gave a sigh of relief when the two men passed her by with only a nod in response to Mrs. Chadwell's hopeful expression. She was thankful her stepmother did not have an acquaintance with either of them, or she might have intercepted them. It wouldn't be the first time that some hapless young man wandered too close and found himself trapped into dancing with Emma before he could gracefully excuse himself.

2

So far this evening, anyone Mrs. Chadwell knew had stayed far away from her web, much to Emma's relief. Dancing at one of these affairs was even worse than sitting. Invariably her partner was young, gauche, and several inches shorter than Emma. As they stumbled about the room Emma was certain everyone noticed the ridiculous frills and ruffles that clung to every inch of her gown.

A furious dig of her stepmother's elbow into her side drew Emma's attention, and she was horrified to see Lord Atherton and Mr. Fairchild approaching with Lady Sylvester.

"There she is, the one in the pale-pink gown."

"Richard, you must be jesting!"

"Not at all, James. Not at all. She is exactly what I am looking for."

The two gentlemen, considered by many to be two of the most eligible bachelors in London Society, paused in one corner of the ballroom so that Mr. Fairchild might make known his chosen bride to his friend, Lord Atherton.

"You set out looking for a lady with no countenance, incredibly bad taste in her gowns, and a family that is known for its spendthrift ways? Your years in India must have affected your brain! Too much sun, you know."

In the same bored tones, Mr. Fairchild replied casually, "My friend, the young lady comes highly recommended by my godmother, Lady Sylvester, one of the arbiters of taste among the *haut ton*."

"Don't believe it," Lord Atherton snorted. "She's trying to gammon you . . . or mayhap pay off an old debt. Perhaps the girl's mother is blackmailing Lady Sylvester. Must be something like that. Damn it, Richard, you can pick and choose from all the beauties. Why would you tie your apron strings to a creature like that?"

"Ah, now you have discovered the point, James. I have no intention of, as you so quaintly put it, tying my apron strings to my future wife."

"But Richard, no need to go that far, just because you don't want to live in her pocket. Just think of seeing her scowling face every morning."

There was an impatient sigh from his companion. "James, will you listen? I do not intend to face the woman over the breakfast table, or at any other time, unless I choose to do so to enquire after the progress of the child. Even Miss Chadwell would be bearable for a short period of time."

"But what about an heir? I mean, your child is a girl. Don't you want a son? And wouldn't it be more, er, enjoyable if you selected one of the many beauties vying for your charms?"

There was a mirthless smile on Mr. Fairchild's face. "Thank you, James. I suspect there are so many because the women you turn down naturally fall to me."

Lord Atherton was handsome, he modestly admitted, but he knew women were more attracted to his companion than to him. There was something about the ruggedness of Fairchild's features, the unattainable air about him, that had the more adventurous of the London beauties falling at his feet. "Ha! But seriously, Richard, you must consider what you are doing."

"I have considered it, James, or I would not be venturing on such a luckless mission in the first place. My own mother is much too lax with the child. While I have no great interest in her, I refuse to allow her to grow up as her mother. That would weigh too heavily on my conscience. The only answer is to marry someone who will provide some discipline."

"Why not employ a stern governess? My sisters had a dragon who never allowed them to put a foot wrong."

"Because my mother would overrule a governess. I must put someone over my child who will have absolute authority, and the only position from which to do so is that of my wife."

"La, Mr. Fairchild," a soft-voiced young lady said, coming to stand at the gentlemen's side, "Lord Atherton, you have both been strangers to our entertainments much of the Season. To what can we attribute this sudden change?"

Lord Atherton smiled coolly at the young lady. "Miss Harper, good evening. Mr. Fairchild and I could not stay away forever from the brilliant lights of the Season."

"And you, Mr. Fairchild? Are you in agreement with your

friend?" The young lady leaned forward, displaying the décolletage of her muslin gown to greater advantage.

Mr. Fairchild eyed the young woman's brazenly displayed charms before meeting her eyes. "Oh, quite, Miss Harper. There are at least two reasons to attend this evening's entertainment."

Though Miss Harper seemed quite liberal in her idea of a virtuous young woman's behaviour, she was unprepared for Mr. Fairchild's response. With crimson cheeks, she moved away from the man after coldly bidding him adieu.

"Richard, that was rather forward, don't you think? If you are not careful, you will soon have the reputation of a rake."

"If a young lady chooses to act in the manner of a loose woman, then she should be prepared for the treatment such a woman receives."

"Well, you can be sure your chosen bride won't behave in the same manner. I doubt she even knows what attracts a man, much less have the audacity to expose . . . uh, to enhance her appearance."

Mr. Fairchild grinned at his friend's discomfort. "True, James, true. Just one of the many benefits of my choice."

"You are really serious?"

"As serious as I can be. Come, let's find my godmother and ask for an introduction."

When Lady Sylvester was found and her godson's intent disclosed, she protested, "Richard, please, I did not seriously mean you should consider the Chadwell girl. Look at her!"

"I already have, and she is perfect for me," Mr. Fairchild assured his godmother smoothly.

"But, Richard, why? All of the young ladies I have introduced to you have been prettier, better mannered, more graceful . . . some have been diamonds of the Season. Why choose someone as graceless and unfashionable as Miss Chadwell?"

Mr. Fairchild ignored her questions. "Will you present me, ma'am? After all, you did promise my mother you would help me choose a wife."

"Your mother! She will never forgive me," the lady moaned.

"I will tell her it is all my fault, Lady Sylvester. After all,

Mother did not blame you when my first choice was so disastrous."

The lady bristled. "Lady Diana was not a poor choice. Her dowry was magnificent, and she was an outstanding beauty. She . . . she had just not settled down to the quiet country life yet. I'm sure after having her child she would have done so to your satisfaction, Richard."

"We will never know, will we? But it is time for me to choose her replacement, and I have selected Miss Chadwell."

Lady Sylvester studied the young man before her. He was certainly attractive, his tall, broad-shouldered figure needing no padding to make him appear manly. His hazel eyes, sometimes green and sometimes light brown, could be very telling, either with humour or cynicism. At other times, they appeared blank, showing nothing of his thoughts.

It was his auburn hair, however, that distinguished him from the other handsome men in the ballroom. It was not bright enough to be called red, but it could never be judged brown, and it indicated an inner fire that few ever saw. Only once had Lady Sylvester been witness to his temper, when she had called on his wife and interrupted a violent argument, and she hoped to never be so again.

"You are choosing someone exactly opposite to Lady Diana, are you not? That is why you have chosen Miss Chadwell," she guessed, watching the shutters fall over his eyes, giving no hint to his reaction. "Very well, Richard. I will introduce you to the young lady if you make me a promise."

"There are others willing to provide an introduction, Lady Sylvester, without extracting a price."

The coolness in his voice told her she was treading on thin ice, but she continued for his mother's sake. "I am only asking that you court the young lady for a while, and not rush into a marriage that you might come to regret."

The concern in her words caused Mr. Fairchild to hesitate. He wanted no long, drawn-out courtship, but the lady before him had always been kind to him, and he would not return rudeness for her consideration.

"Very well, ma'am. I will make you this promise. I shall not offer marriage until I am fully satisfied I know the young lady. And I will specify at least four weeks for the engagement."

"If you think you will be able to escape from an engagement with Mrs. Chadwell's stepdaughter, your wits are to let. They are in desperate need of money. That is the only reason the woman has taken on the task of bringing to market such an unpalatable morsel as Miss Emma. Once they have captured you, you will not escape."

When Mr. Fairchild only shrugged his shoulders in response to her warning, Lady Sylvester gave up the fight. "Very well, come with me."

"Are you coming, James?"

"Of course, Richard. I can't let you get caught in this parson's trap if I can help it."

"After you have settled me, Lady Sylvester," Mr. Fairchild suggested with a laugh, "why not have a go with Lord Atherton. He is still romantic enough to be entranced by the lovelies you have been throwing at my head the past few days."

Lord Atherton's look of alarm brought a smile to Lady Sylvester's face, and the trio arrived at their quarry in a pleasant frame of mind.

"Mrs. Chadwell, how nice to see you again. And Miss Chadwell, how are you doing?"

While her stepmother gushed in response to Lady Sylvester's greeting, Emma only nodded her head.

Mr. Fairchild and Lord Atherton watched the young lady closely during the introduction and saw no leap of eagerness in her eyes as two highly eligible bachelors were presented to her. There was no visible expression in her brown eyes. Another nod acknowledged the introductions, but she spoke no words.

"May I have the pleasure of the next dance, Miss Chadwell, if you are not engaged?"

Mrs. Chadwell, ecstatic, accepted for her. "Oh, Mr. Fairchild! How charming of you! Of course my dear little Emma would love to stand up with you! Nothing could give her greater pleasure! Isn't that right, Emma?" she asked with a familiar accompanying jab.

"Yes, Mama," Emma replied, never raising her eyes.

"At least she can speak," Lord Atherton whispered in his friend's ear as he stared at the young woman in fascination. He had witnessed the presentation of several timid, coun-trified young ladies in past Seasons, but none as shy as Miss Chadwell.

Mr. Fairchild's lips quivered at his friend's comment, since it only echoed his own thought, but he gave no response. The orchestra finished playing a dance, and Richard held out his hand.

"Shall we, Miss Chadwell?"

The young lady rose and placed her hand in his, but Mr. Fairchild received neither a look nor a smile. He led her onto the floor to a set made up of some of the most popular belles of the Season. Though there were whispers and snick-erings when they joined them, Richard knew no one would say him nay.

It was a study in contrast to compare the young women making up the set. Three of the young ladies were elegantly turned out, all smaller than Miss Chadwell, with their hair in luxurious curls decorated with expensive tidbits.

Miss Chadwell showed none of that style. The pink gauze evening gown had too many ruffles, each enhanced by Bel-gian lace that set ill with the rest of the dress. And the colour did not become the young lady wearing it. Her hair, an indeterminate colour, had presumably begun the eve-ning in curls but now flew in every direction, giving her the appearance of a mop. All in all, the picture Miss Chadwell presented was not enticing.

As they proceeded through the measures of the dance, Mr. Fairchild was surprised to find the young woman mov-ing gracefully, not stepping on his toes once. With such encouragement, he said, "Is this your first Season, Miss Chadwell?"

The young woman who danced on the other side of Mr. Fairchild giggled, and Emma's cheeks burned.

"No, I have attended a London Season once before."

"Ah, then you must feel quite at home in London."

"No."

Her bald statement resulted in more giggles. Mr. Fairchild gave the offender a cold stare that brought her humour to an abrupt end.

"You prefer the country, Miss Chadwell?"

"Yes."

Mr. Fairchild asked no more questions, and Emma, though she felt a moment's regret at treating him so shabbily, hoped he was discouraged. She wanted no part of Mr. Fairchild or any other London dandy.

When the dance ended, he escorted her to her stepmother's side. The woman exhibited all the triumph missing from Emma's face.

"My, how delightful a couple you make, Mr. Fairchild! Why, with Emma's height, there aren't too many men who show her off to such advantage."

Emma settled in her chair with a sense of relief, keeping her eyes focused on her hands, clasped tidily in her lap. Unfortunately, Mr. Fairchild did not take her hint.

"I was wondering if Miss Chadwell would care to go for a drive in the park with me tomorrow. If the weather holds, it should be a pleasant afternoon."

"Oh! I'm sure she is honoured, Mr. Fairchild. Aren't you, Emma, love?" her stepmother asked, prompting her with her elbow once more.

Though she glared at the urbane, handsome man standing before her, she said numbly, "Yes, Mr. Fairchild." *Drat the man! What did I do to possibly make him want more of my company?*

"Excellent. I will call for you at three, Miss Chadwell, if that is convenient?"

"She'll be ready and waiting, Mr. Fairchild."

After Mr. Fairchild strolled away, Mrs. Chadwell and her stepdaughter departed from the ball. She knew Emma would achieve no better partner, and even she did not expect Mr. Fairchild to request a second dance. But there was the drive in the park on the morrow.

The lady had a great deal to think about. There was the choice of Emma's dress. The child had no sense of fashion at all. Left to herself, she would choose one of the plain dresses she wore in the country. Then there was her hair. Mrs. Chadwell sighed.

Visions of her own daughter's golden curls floated before her eyes. Her hair was always perfection itself, inspiring poetry from the young bucks who chased after her. Ah, well, Emma couldn't compare to Aurora in any way. What a disappointment the child was.

Emma, tired, sat beside her stepmother in the carriage with her head leaning back against the seat. She, too, thought about the ride in the park. She had intended to use that time to write Handley, her estate manager, or rather her brother's manager. Now she would have to get up early to accomplish that task before her stepmother went into action.

She knew what was ahead of her. Once before when Mrs. Chadwell had caught the scent of a possible suitor, she had become a veritable whirlwind, destroying any pleasure Emma had in London. There were no more museum visits, no time to visit the lending library to borrow the books about the latest farming methods.

Just yesterday, she had discovered a treatise on breeding horses, discussing proper feed, exercise, and training. It included several ideas she had not yet tried on her brother's stock, and she was eager to study it. Now there would be no time for such worthwhile efforts until she had discouraged Mr. Fairchild from any more invitations.

= 2 =

"SIT STILL, EMMA! Monsieur Henri cannot possibly do anything with your hair unless you cooperate."

"Madame," the small man with flamboyant dress and a mincing gait pleaded, "Mademoiselle's hair is not suited to the style you have chosen. If you would allow me to smooth it back into a lover's knot atop the head, I believe—"

"No, no, no! I have told you before, M. Henri, you must dress Miss Chadwell's hair in the height of fashion. That style is too plain. Mr. Fairchild is known for his discriminating taste."

Which makes us all wonder why he is wasting his time on me. Emma sighed. The first time her stepmother had hired the diminutive Frenchman, known as the best hairdresser in the *ton*, to dress her hair, they had had the same argument, and, as always, Mrs. Chadwell won because it was she who would pay the bill—eventually.

Emma knew the hairdresser was right in what would become her. But since she had no interest in snaring a husband, she allowed her stepmother full rein. After all, even though the other style suited her better, nothing would turn her into a raving beauty.

When the hairdresser had departed, leaving Emma's hair looking like a wig someone had plopped down on her head, Mrs. Chadwell turned to the next stage of preparation.

"Now, Emma, I have looked through your closet and have chosen the gown you are to wear. This buttercup-yellow dress with the brown braid trim will be perfect. You will have everyone staring at you in admiration."

11

Emma marvelled once again at her stepmother's blindness. However, she made no demur about the dress. If nothing else, the fact that it was not *comme il faut* to put ruffles on walking dresses saved her from resembling a figure of fun for all who saw her, even if the colour made her look washed out. "Yes, Mama."

"Emma!" the woman exclaimed in exasperation. "Can you not show a little more enthusiasm? I declare, you are such a disappointment to me after my own dear Aurora. Why, when she attracted the most eligible bachelors of the Season, she was so excited, so vibrant. And there you sit like a lump of dough. Don't you think Mr. Fairchild is handsome?"

"Yes, Mama, he is handsome."

"Well, then, show a little animation. And when you are driving in the park, be sure to sit up straight and smile a lot. And don't forget to . . ."

Emma, long used to her stepmother's strictures, returned her thoughts to the book on horse breeding. She had made remarkable strides in one so young in the management of their estate. After one Season in her stepsister's shadow, she had been left at home for the two years after her father's death whenever her family returned to London. Though she missed her father, she'd been relatively happy managing the estate until her stepmother insisted she come to London.

The first year after her father's death, her family had observed the activities of the *ton* from afar, unable to participate because of their mourning. The next year, her stepsister, Aurora, had been relaunched with all the fanfare they could afford.

In spite of all the praise Mrs. Chadwell heaped on her daughter, her marriage had not been brilliant. She had married an earl, true, but after only two years of marriage, Aurora had complained to her mother that they were as near to bankruptcy as before. The earl had yet to make good on some of his promises in the marriage settlement.

Since Emma's brother, Charlie, had celebrated his sister's marriage with outrageous spending, including a new curricle that he had promptly wrecked, there was little money.

Once Aurora had married, Mrs. Chadwell retreated to the country before the bill collectors could dun them.

Emma spent the two years increasing the production of the estate and launching a scheme to improve the bloodlines of her father's stables. When her stepmother insisted it was her turn to try to restore the family wealth by making a brilliant marriage, Emma didn't tell Mrs. Chadwell that she would have better success by staying home and planting a new crop in the south field. She hoped her stepmother would agree by the end of the Season.

"Emma! Are you listening to me?"

"Yes, Mama."

"You must—"

Emma was saved by a rap on the door.

"Come in," commanded Mrs. Chadwell.

A young maid opened the door. "Ma'am, Mr. Chadwell would like to speak with you."

"Well, of course, send my son up at once. I wonder what Charlie wants," Mrs. Chadwell said after the maid had departed. "I hope he will stay until—"

"Hello, Ma, Emma," Charles Chadwell greeted his family as he entered the room, sending all other thoughts from his mother's mind.

"Charlie, we have not seen you for ages! How are you, dear boy?"

"Fine, Ma, fine. And Emma? How are you doing?"

"I am well, Charlie."

"Good, good. I'm glad to hear it."

"Oh, Charlie, you'll never guess who is taking your sister for a carriage ride today! She has done so well!"

"Not Mr. Peterson?" Charlie asked, naming a widower of some sixty-odd years who had shown a slight preference for Emma. He would have gladly danced at the wedding in spite of the difference in Emma's and his age, too, except that Mr. Peterson was not well to let.

"No, of course not! Would I be excited about him?" his mother demanded archly.

"Might be if you were hoping to unload the old girl. Oh, sorry, Emma."

Emma accepted her brother's remarks with amused tolerance. He was completely spoilt and selfish, but she could never forget the wonder she had felt at almost three years of age when she first saw her baby brother.

"Charlie, what a tease you are!" Mrs. Chadwell giggled like a young girl. "You will be so surprised. It is Mr. Fairchild!"

"What? Fairchild? The one who made a fortune in India and then married that heiress?"

"Yes! That's the one. Now, aren't you proud of your sister?"

"Damn proud," Charlie assured his mother while staring at his sister as if to see if she had changed overnight.

"Charlie! Your language!"

"Sorry, Ma. I'm overset by your brilliant matchmaking," he said, leaning over to kiss her cheek. He had always known how to turn his mother up sweet.

Emma said nothing. She intended this to be the last invitation Mr. Fairchild would offer her, and there would be no brilliant marriage to save the family finances, but it would be fruitless to say so.

"When is he coming?"

"At three, which is a little earlier than I would've thought, but perhaps it means they will take a longer drive."

"That is terrific news. By the way, Ma . . . have you any blunt you could lend me? I'm in a bit of a tight spot."

Emma knew they had now reached the reason for her brother's visit. Generally, he ignored his family until they could be of some service to him.

"Oh, Charlie, I have almost nothing until next week. We get the interest from what little we have in the funds then. Could you not wait?"

"Come on, Ma. You won't need it until then. The shopkeepers won't stop serving you, and you can put anyone else off for a week."

"As could you," Emma murmured, only to receive a frown from her young brother.

"Well, all right, dear, I suppose you are right. Just a moment and I'll go get my purse." After the door closed,

Emma turned to her brother. Before she could speak, however, he said, "Make sure you don't let this one get away, Emma." His jolly grin covered a frown.

"Charlie," Emma said urgently, "do not count on Mr. Fairchild to finance your careless spending. You must stop frittering away your inheritance."

"Emma, you have no right to talk to me like that. After all, I am the man of the house."

Emma could not hold back a smile at his claim, but it was tinged with sadness. "I know you are, love, but the estate cannot afford your reckless spending."

"Oh, come on, Emma, you know nothing about it."

"I know everything about it. The bills are still coming in from last Season. If you are not careful, the estate will be sold out from under us." The fear in Emma's voice was ignored by her brother.

"Listen, Emma—"

"Now, Charlie, you must be sure to make this last, because it is all I have until next week, dear boy," his mother said cooing as she reentered the room.

"Of course, Ma. You know how careful I am with what little we have," he said sweetly, sending a triumphant glare to his sister. "Besides, now that our Emma has caught the eye of Mr. Fairchild, I'm sure we'll all be well provided for."

Emma turned her back on her brother and refused to respond to his sally. He knew her feelings about the attempt to marry her off, and he couldn't resist that dig since she'd tried to reason with him. To Mrs. Chadwell, Charlie could do no wrong, and Aurora cared about no one but herself. Only Emma ever tried to curb his reckless spending.

"I think I hear a carriage!" Mrs. Chadwell said as she rushed to the window that looked down upon the quiet street. "Yes! He's here! I shall go down and receive him, Emma. You wait until the maid comes for you. Charlie! You come down with me. It will impress Mr. Fairchild to see us as a united family."

Richard Fairchild was not looking forward to his afternoon appointment. In his logical approach to his problem, it seemed a simple enough matter to choose an unattractive young woman, used to the country, and offer marriage. Then, after the ceremony, he could move her to his country estate and leave her in charge of his daughter, returning himself to town. But the actual carrying out of his plan was proving to be a bore.

He did not want to attend the parties or to waste his afternoons driving slowly around Hyde Park in order that all might see his courtship. In truth, he did not want a courtship, only a wife to care for his child.

While he could cold-bloodedly make such a plan, however, carrying it out in the same fashion demanded that he remain insensitive to the young lady's feelings. Otherwise, his conscience, something he had tried to keep buried since his disastrous marriage, would rise up and trip him.

It was that same determined conscience that was insisting he do something about his daughter. She was a reminder of an unhappy time in his life, and he had rather leave her to others. But when he had returned home for a brief visit at Christmas, he was appalled by her poor behaviour.

He arrived at the Chadwells at the appointed time, giving the reins to his tiger, Jem. "Take them around the square once or twice, Jem. I doubt that the lady will be ready."

"Yes, sir," the lad agreed with a cheeky grin. His master didn't often waste time paying social calls. He was curious about the reason for this one.

Mr. Fairchild was shown into the front parlour and found Mrs. Chadwell and her son awaiting him. He had a nodding acquaintance with Charles Chadwell, but the young man was part of a much younger, and quite wild, crowd.

"Mrs. Chadwell, Mr. Chadwell, good afternoon."

"Mr. Fairchild! Why, is it that time already? I vow, I had almost forgotten your drive with little Emma. I would have, too, had it not been for Emma's excitement. She is so thrilled by your invitation."

Thinking back to the stolid expression evidenced by the young lady at the time of his invitation, Mr. Fairchild found the woman's words hard to believe.

"I'm gratified, Mrs. Chadwell. Is Miss Chadwell ready?"

"Oh, I'm sure she is. Emma is always so prompt. She'll just be adding a few last-minute touches to enchant you, don't you know?" Rising from the sofa, Mrs. Chadwell gave the bell rope a pull and returned to her seat, prepared to entertain her stepdaughter's beau.

"You, of course, know Charlie, Emma's brother. Such a devoted son and brother. He is quite pleased that you are taken with Emma. She has so many wonderful qualities, doesn't she, Charlie?"

"Hmmm? Oh, yes, of course. By the way, Fairchild, who made that coat? That's all the crack, and I'd like one like it."

Mr. Fairchild eyed the young man across from him and discovered his opinion of him had not changed. He murmured, "Weston."

"Charlie, how can you think of coats when other things are more important. Such a silly boy." Mrs. Chadwell giggled.

Fortunately for Mr. Fairchild's patience, Emma appeared at the door.

"There! Did I not tell you she was prompt, Mr. Fairchild? Emma, child, did you bring a shawl? There is a slight chill still in the air, you know."

Emma responded expressionlessly, "Yes, Mama."

Mr. Fairchild stared at the young woman. Somehow he had convinced himself that her behaviour the past evening had been caused by nervousness at a large gathering.

"Well, then, shall we go, Miss Chadwell?" he said with false enthusiasm.

"Yes, of course."

That colourless voice was beginning to irritate him.

Emma sat tensely beside the handsome man. She must convince him to abandon her for another young lady, any other young lady. Not that she thought he wanted her company. He was probably making sport of her.

Whatever his reasons, he was ruining her life. As long as her mother and brother thought there was a possibility of attracting Mr. Fairchild, she would have no peace.

"It is a lovely day, isn't it, Miss Chadwell?"

She pressed her lips together and remained silent.

She saw him turn to look at her out of the corner of her eye, but he was forced forward again when a young man on horseback shouted at him to watch where he was going.

In a slightly less tolerant voice, he tried again. "This must remind you of the country."

Emma stared straight ahead, hating what she was doing but determined to carry through.

"You did say you prefer the country to the city?"

Her response was a nod, nothing more.

"Miss Chadwell, I am making a great effort at polite conversation, but it appears to me I am the only one doing so."

Her stepsister Aurora was a great conversationalist, saying whatever one wanted to hear, caring nothing for the truth. Better to be silent.

Her escort appeared to lose his patience. With an angry voice, he said, "The rumours that you are a half-wit must be true."

Emma's cheeks flooded with colour. She knew the other young people made fun of her, but she had no idea they thought her simple.

With a sigh, Mr. Fairchild said, "I apologise, Miss Chadwell. That was ungentlemanly of me. I'm afraid your lack of response aroused my temper."

Though she was guilty of poor behaviour, she felt she'd received her punishment from his words. "Shall we return home now, Mr. Fairchild?"

Firm hands pulled the frisky pair to a slow walk, and she could feel the man turn towards her. "No, we shall not. But I am relieved to know you can speak."

Why couldn't he just take her home? That's all she wanted.

"Young lady, what kind of a game are you playing?"

"I don't know what you mean, Mr. Fairchild."

"Yes, you do. I do not believe your reticence is sparked by shyness, Miss Chadwell. There was too much coolness in your words. Are you—no, you could not possibly love someone else, or you would take more care with your appearance."

Emma's cheeks flamed at that personal remark.

"Ah, so there is some vanity beneath your wretched appearance."

Emma threw back her shoulders and raised her chin. She would not be beaten down by the comments of some London dandy. Let him say what he would. Soon she would be back at her beloved home, far from London Society.

His hand caught her chin and pulled her face towards him. "Why are we playing these charades? I do not believe your silence is from shyness or stupidity."

"I would like to return home, Mr. Fairchild," Emma said stiffly, keeping her lashes lowered to veil the anger in her eyes.

"Don't you want to complete our drive? Allow yourself to be seen with me?"

His arrogance was too much. "No, Mr. Fairchild, I never wanted to come for a drive with you, nor to dance with you, or . . . or engage in social chitchat."

"You did not want to come for a drive with me?" Mr. Fairchild asked in a mixture of disbelief and anger.

"No, sir. I would like to go home."

Tight-lipped, the man beside her said, "Very well, Miss Chadwell. I will return you to the waiting arms of your family."

Swinging his curricle around in a manoeuvre that caused several hitches in the ever-increasing parade of the *ton*, Mr. Fairchild sprang his spirited greys and headed back to her home. No words were spoken by either party.

Fortunately for Emma, her stepmother had called on a number of her friends to spread the wondrous news that her daughter had attracted the likes of Richard Fairchild and was not at home to observe her stepdaughter's early return. She did not even question Emma about her outing with Mr. Fairchild. The truth was not a necessity to her dreams of the future.

Emma, on the other hand, having achieved her goal of putting Mr. Fairchild off whatever idea had caused him to invite her in the first place, dealt in reality. And the reality of Mr. Fairchild's words hurt.

She had not opposed her stepmother's dressing of her

because she did not want to attract a husband. She wanted to return to the country and resume her duties as manager of her brother's estate. In her logical mind, the best way to achieve that goal was to attract no one. While she could sometimes withstand her family over minor items because of their respect for her ability to provide them with more income, she knew a marriage would be forced upon her if it would be financially beneficial to the others. If she were prevented from managing the estate, she would have to marry or starve.

Mr. Fairchild, however, had made her role even more difficult by forcing her to hear what she had suspected was being said all along. A half-wit with hair resembling a bird's nest, dressed as a creature of fun in her ridiculously ruffled gowns, was not a description to give peace of mind.

That evening, forced to attend another boring entertainment, Emma decided it was time to assert her own taste. She would never be a beauty like her stepsister, but there was no need to give others something to laugh at.

She inspected the gowns her stepmother had thought necessary for her Season and almost abandoned her project. The wardrobe seemed crammed full of ruffles. Only one dress was reasonably plain, but that was a white muslin with pale pink trim. She rang the bell for her maid, actually her nursery maid from long ago now serving her in this capacity to save the expense of a lady's maid.

"Nancy," Emma said as the woman entered, "I need your assistance."

"Well, now, Miss Emma, you know I'll do what I can."

"I don't know if either of us can do enough to accomplish what I want. Do you remember that dress of Mama's, the brilliant green with the bright blue ribbon?"

"That I do. Enough to scare the birds away when she wore it to that picnic."

Emma smiled in remembrance, giving her face a soft glow that had been noticeably absent in public. "I know. It was horrible. But do you know what she did with it?"

"Oh, yes. She brought it with her, in case there was a need for it. But she hasn't wore it since."

"Do you think you could bring it here without her knowing?"

"Maybe. What are you planning to do, Miss Emma?"

"I'm going to look like myself this evening, Nancy, instead of a figure of fun. I am going to use that blue ribbon to replace the pink trim on this white dress, and I am going to dress my hair in a simple style and . . . and I'm going to wear the aquamarine drop Father gave me for my sixteenth birthday."

"Well, glory be, I'd be that glad for you to show everyone how nice you can look."

"Oh, Nancy," Emma giggled with tears in her eyes, "I'm not hoping for nice. I'm just hoping people will stop laughing at me."

The old woman took the younger one in her arms and gave her a hug, taking Emma back to her nursery days.

"Will you help me, Nancy?"

"Why, course I will, child. I'll get Lucy to help, too. That child is right handy with a needle."

"Only if she has time. I don't want her getting into trouble from helping me."

"Don't worry, child. We'll turn you out fine as five pence."

= 3 =

WHEN EMMA DESCENDED the stairs that evening to accompany her stepmother to Lady Stanhope's musicale, she felt a stir of excitement that had been absent the other evenings she had ventured into Society.

Tonight, she knew she looked her best. She would never equal her stepsister's appearance, but she was not a figure of fun. The white muslin had been trimmed in ribbon a clear blue color that accented the sleeves, the low neckline, the deep ruffle that flanked the bottom of the skirt, and tied into a pretty bow beneath the bustline, emphasising Emma's slender figure.

Nancy had drawn her hair back from her face and curled it into an intricate knot on top of her head. It revealed her oval face with high cheekbones and gave her an elegance of which she was unaware. White flowers formed a circlet around the knot, and she wore the aquamarine drop, her last gift from her father. With the excitement, there was a sense of pride as well that manifested itself in her lifted chin and shoulders.

Unfortunately, her stepmother was waiting for her at the foot of the stairs. "Emma! What have you done to yourself! You look terrible! And what are you wearing? I sent word you were to wear the pink organza, not that plain thing! You might as well tell everyone right off that we have no money. They will all know it when they see the way you are dressed. And your hair! Where are those curls that are so fashionable? I cannot believe this. Go back upstairs at once and prepare yourself properly!"

With a calm smile, Emma said, "No, Mama. I am going as I am now or not at all."

"Don't be ridiculous! I am your mother!"

"I know, Mama, but I have let you have the dressing of me long enough. What was suitable for Aurora is not for me. I can never be pretty like her, and you make me a figure of fun dressing me in what suits my stepsister."

"Well," her stepmother huffed. "I have tried to do my best. If you want to go out into public like that, I shall simply tell everyone you chose to do so. Then they will not blame me for having such a disappointing daughter."

No more words were spoken between the two until their arrival at Lady Stanhope's. "Don't expect me to stand by you if you refuse to accept my guidance. I shall enjoy myself and forget all about you," the older woman warned.

"Very well, Mama."

"Hmph!" Mrs. Chadwell snorted. "Well, no one will confuse you with Aurora this evening. *She* would never have ignored my guidance and appeared in public like that!"

"It is not likely that anyone would have mistaken me for Aurora in any case, Mama, unless they were blind."

Mrs. Chadwell left the carriage and, without waiting for her stepdaughter to descend, moved to the entrance of Lady Stanhope's home as if she were alone.

Emma gave a rueful shrug and followed in her wake.

Emma was uncomfortable. She knew that her stepmother was doing what she thought was best for her. But Mrs. Chadwell's desire to find a rich husband for Emma was the opposite of Emma's decision to remain in the country, managing her brother's estate. Now, here she sat, all alone. Usually her stepmother left Emma near the chaperones when she went to play cards.

"It's your own fault," she reminded herself. She was the one who had dug in her heels, made no effort to meet people, allowed her stepmother the dressing of her. Poor Mama! Emma chuckled to herself. She had no idea what to do with a long Meg like herself.

Out of the corner of her eye, she saw Mr. Fairchild, but

she knew the gentleman wouldn't speak to her this evening. With a sigh, she stared straight ahead.

"Why, Miss Chadwell," a familiar voice called.

Looking up, Emma saw Miss Harper strolling by on the arm of one of her many gallants. With a reserved smile, Emma greeted the young woman, though she had no liking for her.

"What is wrong? Has even your mother had enough of your company?" Miss Harper trilled before whispering something to her partner that caused him to laugh uproariously.

Emma was stunned by such malice, but before she could pull herself together to respond, if indeed there was a suitable response, the seat beside her was filled.

"Miss Chadwell, I have been looking for you. I enjoyed our ride in the park this afternoon so much. Good evening, Miss Harper, Mr. McDonald."

Emma knew the superiority she felt was wrong when Miss Harper gave a sniff of anger as she greeted Mr. Fairchild and hurried away, but she enjoyed it anyway. It also reminded her that she was undeserving of his protection. "Thank you, Mr. Fairchild. Your rescue was more than I deserved."

"It is of no matter, Miss Chadwell. Her insult was more than you deserved also. I think they cancel each other."

Though she smiled gratefully, Emma kept her eyes lowered. In spite of his reassurance, her earlier behaviour was an embarrassment to her. To be paid back with such kindness was overwhelming.

"I just happened to be strolling nearby," Mr. Fairchild continued. "But where is your mother? Surely you did not come without her?"

"No. No, my stepmother is in the drawing room playing cards."

"And she has abandoned you? That's not quite *comme il faut*," Mr. Fairchild protested.

Emma, with a rueful grin, looked at her companion for the first time since he sat down. "In all honesty, Mr. Fairchild, it is my fault. You see, Mama is angry with me, and it is her way of teaching me a lesson."

His eyes were kind as he looked at her. "Even so, it leaves you open to insults such as the one you just sustained. Your stepmother should be beside you."

"Perhaps, but you are being generous in not reminding me it is what I deserve." She read surprise in his face. The Emma Chadwell he had met earlier would not have admitted guilt. In fact, she would not have spoken at all. "I owe you my thanks."

The musicians began tuning their instruments, and Emma said, "I believe they are ready to begin the performance, so I will excuse you to find your chair."

His eyebrows raised, Mr. Fairchild asked, "Am I not welcome to keep this seat, Miss Chadwell? Perhaps you were waiting for a friend?"

Emma's cheeks flushed a bright red. With her eyes trained on her hands, she said, "I was trying to politely excuse you from my company. It is not fair to pay you back for your assistance by forcing you to remain at my side all evening."

She bravely raised her gaze to his, expecting him to bid her adieu. Instead, after a thoughtful survey of her face, he said, "Allow me to make you my compliments on your appearance this evening. You look enchanting."

A low chuckle escaped Emma. "I believe you are exceeding the requirements of gentlemanly behaviour, sir," she protested, "though I do appreciate it."

After his momentary surprise, Mr. Fairchild returned her smile. "I meant what I said, Miss Chadwell. And I believe I owe you an apology for my remarks this afternoon."

Before Emma could respond, Lady Stanhope stood up in front of her guests to introduce the entertainment for the evening, and all conversation was ended.

Emma could not help but be aware of her companion during the performance. Not only did Mr. Fairchild make several humourous remarks about the singer, but he drew the attention of others. Used to being ignored, Emma found the stares of the *ton* unnerving.

The soprano came to the end of the aria and indicated she would now take a rest, leaving her audience free to seek out refreshment.

Emma fidgeted in her chair, unsure of her course of action. She could not return to playing the sullen, silent Miss Chadwell of previous evenings, not after Mr. Fairchild's kindness to her. Yet, as she realised during the music when members of Society took note of their friendliness, she didn't want to promote her mother's ridiculous belief that Mr. Fairchild would offer for her.

"Are you uncomfortable, Miss Chadwell?"

"No, of course not," she said quickly, keeping her gaze on her hands.

"Perhaps it is my company you object to?" There was a teasing note in his voice that invited a smile, but Emma could not respond.

"I suppose I am wrong to think we are dealing better with each other in the wake of our carriage ride."

Her brown eyes flashing up at him, Emma fought to control the colour filling her cheeks. "I owe you an apology for my behaviour this afternoon, Mr. Fairchild. I was trying—that is, you don't understand what—" Emma gave up. She did not know how to explain her situation to this attractive stranger.

"You are right, Miss Chadwell, I do not understand. Was it such a terrible thing to ask you to drive with me?"

His lightly asked question was such a contrast to the difficulties she faced that Emma could not keep back an honest answer. "Yes. Yes, it was."

Before the frowning Mr. Fairchild could demand an explanation, they were interrupted by Mrs. Chadwell.

"Why, Mr. Fairchild. How kind of you to keep my little Emma company."

Emma stiffened, but the man beside her answered amicably, "It is my pleasure, Mrs. Chadwell."

"I hope you will excuse my child's appearance this evening. I don't know what got into her head, because she rejected the most beautiful gown to appear in that dowdy old thing and wouldn't even have her hair dressed in the latest fashion. I vow I have never seen her look less stylish."

"I find her appearance charming, Mrs. Chadwell."

Emma sat silently, hoping her mother would not embarrass her further.

"Well, that's all right, then. Not that Emma dressed only to please you," the woman assured Mr. Fairchild with a knowing look, "but I would hate for you to hold her lack of taste against her."

Emma inserted hurriedly, "Mama, would you like to depart now? I have a headache from—from the music."

"Nonsense, child. The evening is still young. Besides," Mrs. Chadwell added with a frown, "I am down three pounds and must have an opportunity to recoup my losses."

"I will be happy to keep an eye on your daughter, Mrs. Chadwell, so you may have no worries about her safety while you are concentrating on the cards."

"There now, if that is not exactly what I had in mind, Mr. Fairchild, only I hesitated to ask. You are a perfect gentleman."

"Thank you, madam," Mr. Fairchild said graciously, though Emma thought she detected an ironic tone in his voice.

Mrs. Chadwell beamed at the man. "Well, since I can leave my little Emma in your care, Mr. Fairchild, I shall recoup my losses." She strolled away with a triumphant look on her face.

"I am sorry, sir," Emma said stiffly.

"Whatever for, Miss Chadwell?"

"You are aware . . . she had no right to . . ."

"Good evening, Miss Chadwell. Would you care for some ratafia?" Lord Atherton asked, surprising the couple.

Emma smiled up at the gentleman, knowing his presence would keep Mr. Fairchild from asking any awkward questions. "Thank you, my lord. I would love something to drink."

In spite of Mr. Fairchild's scowl, Lord Atherton handed her a cup and sat down on the other side of her. "Are you enjoying the music, Miss Chadwell?" he asked.

"Yes, thank you, Lord Atherton. I find the music delightful."

"Does that mean you also are musically inclined?" the gentleman asked politely.

"Only as an appreciator of it, Lord Atherton. After my stepsister's skilful execution, I'm afraid my attempts discouraged both my stepmother and my teacher."

"Brava," Mr. Fairchild inserted. "We need more audience and fewer mediocre performers."

"Surely you are not classifying Signora Signatore as a mediocre performer?" Miss Chadwell asked in astonishment.

"No, I had some of our young friends in mind. In fact," Mr. Fairchild said, watching Miss Chadwell closely, "I'm afraid I would classify your stepsister in that category."

"Richard!" Lord Atherton protested.

Emma stared at the man beside her before turning to his friend. "Do not be alarmed, Lord Atherton. Mr. Fairchild has judged her talent correctly. But, I beg you, don't make such an assessment in front of my stepmother, Mr. Fairchild."

He offered her a warm smile for her honesty. "Have no fear, Miss Chadwell. I am coming to understand your step-mother very well. It was your appearance that made her angry with you, was it not?"

In spite of her blush that confirmed his guess, Emma had no intention of admitting anything to him. "I beg your pardon, Mr. Fairchild, but our argument is between my stepmother and me. I should never have mentioned it."

"Well, of course it is. I don't know what has gotten into Richard this evening, Miss Chadwell. Normally he is the best-mannered of fellows."

"I am sure he is, Lord Atherton. I should share the blame. I believe I tried his patience this afternoon."

"I'm afraid I'm not known for that particular quality my-self, Miss Chadwell," Mr. Fairchild said. "Would you care to try me again?"

"I beg your pardon?"

"Would you care to drive out with me again tomorrow?"

Emma's heart sank. After his rescue, and their friendli-ness during the evening, Mr. Fairchild had every right to expect a positive response. But she could not.

"Thank you, Mr. Fairchild, for your invitation, but I'm afraid I cannot drive out with you tomorrow."

"Why?"

"Richard, what are you doing? Don't badger Miss Chadwell."

"James, this is a private conversation. Why do you not leave the two of us alone?"

"No! No, please, Lord Atherton. We have nothing to dis-cuss privately. Please do not abandon me."

Though Lord Atherton was clearly unhappy with the situation, Emma breathed a sigh of relief when he sank back down in his chair.

"I cannot leave the two of you alone, Richard, since Miss Chadwell has asked me to remain."

Mr. Fairchild sighed. "All right, James. Miss Chadwell, would you please explain your reluctance to accompany me tomorrow?"

"Richard! It is ungentlemanly to press her if she does not care for your invitation."

With such an able champion, Emma found an answer unnecessary, and she silently blessed Lord Atherton for remaining beside her.

"Are you in love with someone in the country?" Mr. Fairchild asked abruptly.

Startled out of her silence, Emma said, "No! Whatever gave you that idea?"

"You see, James, our theories were not correct. I suspected as much when I saw how you were dressed this evening," he said, smiling at Emma.

"Excuse me," Emma said as she rose from her chair.

"Where are you going?" Mr. Fairchild asked as he stood beside her.

"To find my stepmother."

"You know she does not want to be disturbed. Why can you not answer a simple question? All I want to know is why you are turning down my invitations."

Emma sat back down, trying to ignore the stares of those near them. "Mr. Fairchild—all right. I will tell you why I have refused your invitation, and why I acted as I did this afternoon. I have no interest in matrimony, but my family wishes me to wed. And my foolish stepmother imagines because you offered me one invitation, I will soon be the wealthy Mrs. Fairchild and solve all their financial difficulties. Can you imagine how excited she would become if she knew you offered a second invitation?"

"Are you not in agreement with your stepmother's conclusions?"

"Don't be absurd, Mr. Fairchild. I have no idea why you

asked me to drive with you today. It could be curiosity to see if I am as strange as the *ton* says," she ignored Lord Atherton's gasp and Mr. Fairchild's flushed cheeks, "or it could be to settle a bet, since gentlemen are so fond of gaming. Whatever it was, it has caused a stir in my household, and I see no reason for my discomfort, whatever your reason."

"Would you like to know my reason?" Mr. Fairchild asked.

"No, I would not. I just want to go home."

"Your mother is correct, Miss Chadwell." He smiled at her incredulous stare. "I am looking for a wife, and you are the candidate I have in mind. Does that make it worth your while to accept my invitation?"

Emma stared at her companion, her cheeks aflame, before she came to her senses. Turning away from him, she muttered, "You are making fun of me, Mr. Fairchild. I admit I did not behave well this afternoon, but I do not think I deserve this."

"I am quite serious, Miss Chadwell. I have chosen you as the future Mrs. Fairchild."

An agitated Lord Atherton ignored the private conversation. "It isn't proper to do this in public, Richard. And besides, you must apply to her guardian first!"

"No!"

"That would be your stepmother?" Mr. Fairchild asked calmly, ignoring her protest.

"Please, Mr. Fairchild, please don't . . . I don't wish to marry."

"Then you only have to say no."

"You do not understand!"

During the argument, the soprano had retaken her position before the audience and begun her performance again. Lord Atherton quieted his companions, and all three turned to the music. But their minds did not turn with them.

Emma was in a panic. There was no doubt in her mind that her stepmother would accept Mr. Fairchild's offer, should he be serious. In no time at all, she could find herself married to the stranger beside her. Surely he could not intend to propose. There were so many beautiful young women with large dowries eager to marry him. There was no reason for him to choose her.

When the music ended, Emma, dreading any further conversation with the two men, welcomed the advent of Miss Harper and another young lady, Miss Little. They had come, they sweetly explained, to ask Miss Chadwell if she would care to stroll about the room with them. And, of course, the gentlemen were welcome to join them if they pleased.

Emma recognised their thinly veiled plot, but she saw the opportunity to escape through them. "That is most kind of you," she said, smiling prettily, "and I'm sure the gentlemen will welcome the opportunity to stroll about."

She waited until everyone was standing and the men had indicated their agreement, as they perforce had little choice without offering an insult. Then, looking over their shoulders in the direction of the drawing room, she exclaimed, "Oh, dear, I am sorry. My mother is beckoning me. Perhaps I will be able to join you another time."

Ignoring the glare in Mr. Fairchild's eyes, she smiled regretfully at Lord Atherton. He did not deserve his fate, but she had to escape.

Slipping into the card room, she informed her stepmother that she had an awful headache and that Mr. Fairchild seemed about to leave. Though Mrs. Chadwell was reluctant to depart, having finally found a winning streak, she felt compelled to accede to Emma's plea.

Before she went to bed that evening, Emma determined that it would require greater steps than she had taken to discourage Mr. Fairchild from making sport of her. That had to be his intention, because she could not accept what he had said as the truth.

She had suffered a relapse in her plan because of her own vanity, she admitted. If she had allowed her stepmother full rein over her appearance and continued to sit stolidly, ignoring the insults directed at her, Mr. Fairchild would not have deigned to speak to her again after their afternoon outing. But she had wanted to appear to advantage before him just once, and that had been her downfall.

Why could things not continue as they had until this year? She had been so happy on the estate on her own, directing the various farming activities, studying new theories in farming. She felt sure of herself there, and she was respected by the people around her. She belonged in the country, not here in London as either a Society miss or, should Mr. Fairchild be serious, a matron.

Before finally closing her eyes, she cautioned herself against the uncharitable thought of having received a better offer than her stepsister. If she did not put away such childishness, she would have to give up her life in the country. And that she did not want to do.

= 4 =

WHEN EMMA AROSE the next morning, she found she was already too late. Her world had turned upside down.

"Darling, darling Emma! Wake up at once. Oh, you sly little darling! You didn't even give me one hint last evening. I should be absolutely furious with you, but I will forgive you. How absolutely marvellous. I never dreamed . . . Emma? Wake up at once, you slugabed! You were never used to lie around in the country."

"W-what is it, Mama?" Emma struggled to ask, having been up half the night worrying about her situation.

"What is it, the child asks! Why, you are engaged to the most eligible man! That's what it is, my wonderful darling!"

"What?" Emma asked tersely, throwing back the covers.

"Your brother is downstairs, waiting to wish you happiness. Just as he should. He's such a good boy!"

"Leave me, Mama. I must dress and deal with Charlie. I would not be counting Mr. Fairchild's riches just yet."

"What are you talking about, child?"

Emma ignored the woman as she threw open the wardrobe and drew out a plain day dress she wore frequently in the country. Nancy came through the door as she was struggling into it, demanding, "What's to do, miss? . . . Oh, good morning, ma'am."

"Nancy, choose another dress for Miss Emma. She'll be receiving her betrothed this morning," Mrs. Chadwell announced, preening as if she were responsible for such a coup. Fortunately for her peace of mind, she then left her stepdaughter's bedchamber.

"Forget what she said, Nancy. Just button me up. I must go down and deal with my brother before he puts an announcement in the paper and causes me to be the laughing-stock of the entire world, not just the *ton*."

Nancy pressed her lips firmly together to hold in the questions that were demanding to be asked and did as she was told.

It was only a few minutes later that Emma opened the door to the parlour to discover her brother sitting on the sofa, one leg crossed over the other while he sipped a glass of brandy.

"Drinking so early, brother?"

"Ah, if it is not my very fortunate sister. I believe Mama told you the good news."

"Do not be ridiculous! Whatever Mr. Fairchild said to you, he has no intention of wedding me."

"You are wrong, Emma," the young man said earnestly. "You see, Mama has already signed the settlement and the notice has been sent to the papers."

"But, Charlie, you know I do not wish to marry. Surely you will not force me into a marriage I do not want!" Emma was struggling with her composure. She had never believed Mr. Fairchild to be serious.

Charles Chadwell felt a twinge of guilt, but he firmly thrust it away. "Now, Emma, you know you must eventually marry, and Mr. Fairchild is slap up to the mark. You'll be the envy of all the ladies." He paused before adding, "Besides, he was most generous. All my—our financial problems are over."

"And what will happen when you have spent that money, Charlie, and the estate no longer has anyone to ensure its continued production? Shall you come begging to my husband? I think you have made a poor bargain."

"Come now, Emma. Do you think I will fail in managing my own estate?" he blustered.

"Yes, I do, and I would advise you to set all to rights at once, Charlie, before it is too late."

"But Emma, love, you have not heard all my good news. It is early days yet, but I hope I am to be wed soon. And to an heiress!"

Emma stared at her brother in surprise. She still thought of him as a boy, but she knew better than to say he was too young. "Who, Charlie?"

He dropped his eyes and half turned away as he muttered, "You do not know her. Her father is in trade."

Emma swallowed the words she wanted to say. Her brother looked vulnerable as he stood before her. She approached him and laid a hand on his arm. "Do you . . . do you care for her?"

He looked at her in surprise but then lowered his lashes. Shrugging his shoulders, he muttered, "Of course. And I am not the fool you think me. I know I cannot run the estate as well as you. Nor do I want to be stuck in the country. But when I marry Miss Stokie, I won't have to. I can hire a new manager, who'll probably make the place really pay."

Emma winced, but the young man never knew he had injured her as he continued, "And I can stay in London and enjoy myself."

Grasping at straws, Emma said, "But, Charlie, if you are to be wealthy soon, could I not return to the country? Then, you would not have the expense of hiring a manager."

"Miss Stokie won't want you around, old girl, an unmarried sister."

His careless cruelty cut through Emma's heart. Tears spurted into her eyes and she turned away.

From behind her, Charlie added, "Besides, Fairchild will be generous, and I'll admit the money will come in handy convincing Miss Stokie to accept me."

Several tears slipped from Emma's eyes and trailed down her cheeks. Even if she convinced Mr. Fairchild to withdraw his offer, she was well and truly lost now. Never would she be able to return to her home.

The butler, Walters, instructed by Mrs. Chadwell, led Mr. Fairchild to the parlour and swung wide the doors.

With a gasp, Emma brushed past him to escape upstairs, leaving her brother to make her excuses.

In her chamber, she faced the future with a deep breath, recognising the inevitability of marriage to Mr. Fairchild. Her dream of returning to her brother's estate was shattered.

Dully, she poured some water into the bowl that stood by the window. She must erase all trace of her distress. Unless she was much mistaken, she would be called upon to accept Mr. Fairchild's proposal, and she had already embarrassed herself once today in front of the man. She did not want to do so a second time.

Mr. Fairchild sat in the drawing room with a frown on his face. He would swear the tears Miss Chadwell was shedding were not tears of joy. Nor had her response to his appearance been encouraging. Had he made a mistake? She seemed perfect for his plans, but he did not want an unwilling wife.

The door opened to readmit Mr. Chadwell, who had gone to alert his mother to their guest's arrival. "Emma and my mother will be right down. They are both as happy as can be about your proposal."

"You are sure Miss Chadwell is willing to receive my offer?"

"I'm positive. Why, you're the most sought-after bachelor in all of London. Course she's happy," Charlie assured him even as he crossed his fingers behind his back. "It was just nervousness. You know how high-strung some women are. Not that she ain't healthy as a horse," he hurriedly assured Mr. Fairchild. At his guest's raised eyebrow and cold stare, Mr. Chadwell rephrased his statement. "Emma is . . . is always in good health, sir."

The door swung open again, this time admitting Mrs. Chadwell. "Oh, Mr. Fairchild. What a joy it is to see you. I cannot tell you how delighted I am that you appreciate my little Emma. She is such a treasure."

"I agree, ma'am. I trust she is all right?"

"All right? Why, of course she is."

Mr. Fairchild frowned. "She seemed unhappy when I first arrived."

"Just nerves, my dear man. You know how young women are. And Emma is a most modest child. She finds it difficult to believe that she has caught your eye. After all, you are quite a catch," the woman trilled as she batted her eyes at her future son-in-law.

"Is Miss Chadwell willing to receive me this afternoon so that I may assure her of my desire to marry her?" Mr. Fairchild asked, still uneasy about what had occurred. Perhaps it had been high-handed of him to sign the settlement before proposing, but Miss Chadwell seemed sensible enough to understand the reason for his haste once he'd had a chance to explain.

Smoothing the fat, falsely gold curls that clustered over one ear, Mrs. Chadwell said, "Of course she is. But may I say it is such a joy to welcome you into our little family, Mr. Fairchild. Do you know my daughter? Such a joy to me, and so divinely beautiful. Not that Emma is not also a . . . a joy to me, but she never showed the talent of Aurora. Why, if you had heard her play the pianoforte!"

"Mama! I'm sure Mr. Fairchild don't want to hear about an old married woman. After all, it's Emma he wants."

Mrs. Chadwell appeared startled at her son's words. "Why, of course, Charlie. Didn't I just say that Emma is a joy to me?"

"Perhaps it would be better if I returned later this afternoon to speak with Miss Chadwell. She might like to accompany me for a ride in the park, if she has recovered."

"No, no, Mr. Fairchild. I promise you she will be right down. Charlie, go find what is keeping your sister."

As soon as the young man had left to do his mother's bidding, Mrs. Chadwell leaned forward to say confidentially, "I am glad for this opportunity to talk with you privately, Mr. Fairchild. Emma is such an innocent. I beg you to be patient with her. She . . ."

"I met Emma on the stairs," Charlie said as he opened the door for his sister to precede him into the room.

Emma forced herself to meet Mr. Fairchild's searching glance as she approached him and extended her hand. "Good day, Mr. Fairchild. I beg you will excuse my earlier behaviour."

"Of course, Miss Chadwell." He took her hand and led her to a seat on the sofa before sitting beside her. When the other two in the room gave no indication of departing, Mr. Fairchild said, "May I have a moment of privacy with Miss Chadwell to discuss the matter?"

"Yes, of course," Mrs. Chadwell said, rising and taking her son by the arm.

"Mama, I ain't sure. . . ." Charlie said in an audible whisper that the two on the sofa clearly heard.

"Come now, Charlie." Mrs. Chadwell laughed artificially. "We can trust Mr. Fairchild with our Emma." Over her shoulder, she added, "I will return in a few moments, Emma, dear."

Once the door was closed behind them, Charlie expressed his concerns more clearly. "I ain't sure that's wise, Mama. What if she rejects him? She wasn't too pleased when I told her this morning. Did you talk to her?"

"Yes, I did, Charlie. But it was just the surprise. By the time I reached her room, she had already accepted the engagement. Emma has been difficult about making a good marriage, but I believe she has come around. And you must admit, she has done us proud."

"Yes, if she just goes through with it. I must tell you, Mama, that without that marriage settlement, we will go under. So you just be sure she doesn't reject our gold mine."

Emma sat nervously twisting her hands in her lap, waiting for the silent man beside her to proceed. She almost jumped from the sofa when he reached over to place his large hand over hers.

"Miss Chadwell, I am sure your brother has informed you of my intentions. As I did last night," he added, searching her face for any response.

"I did not believe you last evening, Mr. Fairchild," she said unsteadily.

"Lord Atherton reprimanded me for my disgraceful behaviour, but I have never had much patience for all the rigamarole of Society's rules."

He was encouraged by a quiver of her lips as Miss Chadwell looked up at him. "I suppose I had no need to inform you of that, did I?"

Emma allowed the smile to break through as she agreed with him. "There seem to be a great many of them, doesn't there?"

"Yes, but Miss Chadwell, I truly did not mean to cause

you any distress, and if you oppose our marriage, I will withdraw my offer."

Last night, Emma thought her problems would be solved if Mr. Fairchild did not offer for her. But after talking to Charlie, she realised she would have no home if Mr. Fairchild did not offer. How quickly life could change. "No, Mr. Fairchild. I am grateful of the honour you do me, and I accept your offer."

There was neither enthusiasm nor shyness in her response, and Mr. Fairchild was surprised at his reaction. He wanted neither in his bride, so why was he disappointed? A calm acceptance of his reasonable offer, that was what he wanted and that was what he received.

"Thank you, Miss Chadwell. I am pleased you have accepted me. Perhaps you would like to accompany me on a ride in the park? We have many things to discuss."

But Emma had used all her energy dealing with the changes in her life. "Do you not think it would be better to reserve any discussions for another day? We have . . . had a lot of excitement for one day."

Mr. Fairchild looked sharply at the young woman beside him and noticed how pale her cheeks were. Was he being insensitive to her? "Of course, Miss Chadwell. I had not realised accepting my offer would drain you so."

Emma bit her bottom lip before she attempted to salvage his good humour. "I suspect it is not the acceptance that has drained me, as you so charmingly put it, Mr. Fairchild, but the surprise of your offer. I truly did not think—"

"My apologies, Miss Chadwell. My lamentable manners again. Of course, my proposal was sudden, and you must have time to adjust to it. And to prepare for the onslaught of well-wishers you will receive."

Emma looked surprised. "Oh, no, surely . . . of course, you are correct, sir. When will the announcement appear in the paper?"

"It will be in tomorrow's paper."

"Oh, dear. And you think . . . oh, my."

Mr. Fairchild studied his fiancée's face. Once again he surprised himself by his reactions. He did not want a clinging wife, but he had not realised one as unenthusiastic as Miss Chadwell would injure his pride as much as it did. "Would you prefer we kept our engagement secret?" he asked in sardonic tones.

Recognising treacherous ground, Emma immediately said, "Of course not, Mr. Fairchild. I shall be proud to meet the *ton* as your betrothed."

"Good. And do not let your stepmother have the dressing of you anymore."

Emma's shoulders stiffened, but she maintained a pleasant smile. "I'll inform her of your preferences, sir."

Now it was Mr. Fairchild's turn to feel unsure of himself. "I did not mean . . ."

"I think it is best if I go prepare for the numerous congratulations I shall receive for snaring you, Mr. Fairchild. Perhaps tomorrow we can have the conversation you desired."

"Yes, of course. Until tomorrow."

Emma rose with her guest, ringing for Walters to show him out. Mr. Fairchild stood awkwardly before taking her hand in his. "I am honoured you have accepted my offer, Miss Chadwell."

"Thank you, Mr. Fairchild. I hope you may always be so."

When he left in Walters's company, Emma sank back onto the sofa. It could be worse, she reminded herself. She could be an unwanted spinster in her brother's household. At least she would have her own place as the mistress of Mr. Fairchild's household.

Mr. Fairchild left the Chadwell residence in a state of confusion. He had done what he set out to do. Now he wasn't sure if he was happy. Miss Chadwell was perfect for his plan, and she seemed to understand the kind of marriage he wanted. So why did he want more?

Several evenings later, Lord Atherton stared across the candlelit table beneath lowered lids at his friend, then took a sip of his port. "How is Miss Chadwell? I have not seen her since the announcement of your engagement."

"Nor has anyone else."

"You have not—?"

"Oh, yes, of course, I have visited her every day, but she has not gone out in public."

"Not feeling well?" Lord Atherton asked casually, trying to contain his rampant curiosity.

"No . . . no, she has not been feeling well."

Though he continued to study his friend's drawn face, Lord Atherton asked no more questions. He had been friends with Mr. Fairchild only since the death of his first wife. Others had told him of the changes wrought by his marriage and his wife's death, but Lord Atherton had knowledge only of the calm, cynical handsome man who had been pursued by every matchmaking mama in the *ton*.

One other thing about Mr. Fairchild drew Lord Atherton to him. That was his loyalty to friends and his discretion among some of the world's worst gossips. Lord Atherton hoped he emulated his friend in those respects, but he would not force a confidence from his friend if he did not want to give one.

Lord Atherton was startled from his thoughts by a quiet voice. "Have I made a mistake, James?"

With a sympathetic smile, Lord Atherton said, "How can I say, Richard. I did not think her suitable, but that night at Lady Stanhope's . . .'"

"Ah, yes. That was what convinced me she would be perfect. Intelligent . . . not beautiful and demanding, but reasonably attractive. And understanding."

"She seemed ideal that evening unless . . . unless her ability to understand you would demand too much from your conscience."

"Yes," Mr. Fairchild laughed ruefully, "I did consider that aspect, but I determined that I could control my conscience. After all, many women suffer much worse when they marry."

"So what is the problem, friend?"

"I think she is being forced into the marriage."

"Why do you think that?"

"She does not appear to enjoy my company."

"But you said she was not feeling well. Could that not explain away behaviour, whatever it is?"

"I do not know. Perhaps it is the presence of her mother, but I cannot see her alone, even though we are engaged.

Her mother insists on being present at every meeting. And you know how intrusive that woman is."

"But can you not take Miss Chadwell for a ride in the park? Surely her mother would not insist on accompanying you then."

With a sigh, Mr. Fairchild admitted, "No, that is not possible, at least not yet. Her mother insists she is not recovered enough from her cold to venture out into the sharp weather we have been experiencing."

"Why do you not invite Miss Chadwell, with her mama, of course, to your estate? Your mother could entertain her mama and you could stroll in the shrubbery with Miss Chadwell. Perhaps you might even discover pleasure in her company again. She was most charming at Lady Stanhope's."

"James, you are brilliant! Why did I not think of that? A house party is the very thing. I can introduce her to my mother and the child. You will come, won't you? I may need your support."

Lord Atherton could not refuse his friend, but the prospect of several weeks in Mrs. Chadwell's company did not fill his heart with joy.

"I know, James, I know. But I shall invite a nice young lady as a companion for you. Have you any preferences?"

"Here now! Don't do that," Lord Atherton protested, alarmed even more at being cornered by a young woman with marriage on her mind.

For the first time that evening, Richard Fairchild smiled, feeling much lighter of heart since his friend's suggestion. "Do not worry. I will not ask Miss Harper or her friend, Miss Little. I'll ask my mother to invite someone who'll be kind to Miss Chadwell. If it turns out she doesn't want to marry me, you and I can take our leave and there will be company for her besides her dragon of a mama."

"Are you hoping Miss Chadwell will cry off?" Lord Atherton asked.

Mr. Fairchild avoided his friend's inquisitive gaze. "I am not sure."

= 5 =

MR. FAIRCHILD PAID his customary call on Miss Chadwell the next morning with an enthusiasm that had lately been absent.

"Good morning, Miss Chadwell, Mrs. Chadwell," he greeted them cheerfully. His good humour was lessened somewhat when he discovered that the ladies of the family were not alone. "Ah, greetings to you, also, Chadwell."

"Good day, Mr. Fairchild. It is fine weather we are having, is it not?"

Mr. Fairchild nodded in agreement, then turned from the brother to the sister who had made no verbal agreement. She sat quietly on the sofa, her eyes downcast, her hands folded in her lap. "You are looking well, Miss Chadwell. I believe your cold has almost gone away."

There was a hoarse thank-you, but nothing else. In fact, the young lady looked much as she had every morning, her nose red and her eyes watering. Had he not seen the evidence of her disability, he might have thought her pretending an illness to avoid him, because she showed no enthusiasm for his company.

But fortunately, for the sake of his self-esteem, he could attribute it to the cold from which she was suffering. At least she had adhered somewhat to his request in the matter of her appearance and wore her hair in the elegant style she had adopted at Lady Stanhope's. But she continued to wear the frilly dresses. Mr. Fairchild promised himself that after their marriage, all such clothes would be given to the poor.

"True, she looks quite well this morning," Mrs. Chadwell

chirped. "I declare, ever since your proposal, my little Emma has been a blushing beauty."

That was too much even for her son. "Mama! Don't be ridiculous!" At his mother's glare, he amended, "Emma's well enough. Fairchild ain't blind, and he chose her. No need to puff her up so."

That was the first time Mr. Fairchild found himself in agreement with his future brother-in-law, and probably the last, he told himself.

"I wondered, Mrs. Chadwell, if it would be convenient for you and Miss Chadwell to accompany me to my estate for a week or two. I would like my future wife to see her home and meet my mother and daughter."

For the first time since his arrival, Mr. Fairchild had a glimpse of Miss Chadwell's brown eyes, a spark of interest warming them. "You have a child?" she asked hoarsely, then coughed.

"Did you not know? My apologies, Miss Chadwell. There has been so much talk of my doings, I assumed it was common knowledge."

"Is that not amazing? My little Emma to be a mama already! I had forgotten you had a child, Mr. Fairchild. A little girl, did you say?"

Though he answered her stepmother's question, Mr. Fairchild's eyes remained on the face of his betrothed. "Yes, a little girl. She is . . . uh, four years old."

"A child . . ." Emma whispered, life stirring in her breast once more. The strain of the past week, a combination of her engagement and her illness, had been great. But the thought of a child, someone to whom she could pour out all her love, an emotion for which she was sure Mr. Fairchild had no use, warmed her heart.

"I hope it does not disturb you that I have a child, Miss Chadwell. I should have made sure you were informed of that before I made my offer. If it makes a difference—"

"No! She'll marry you just the same," her brother's tense voice insisted.

"Of course not! She will love your child!" her mother's strident soprano joined in.

44

But it was Emma's response that interested Mr. Fairchild. Beneath the noise of the others, she whispered, "I should be happy to meet your daughter, sir."

Her genuine interest gave Mr. Fairchild encouragement. "Then you will come to Fairchild House for a visit? My mother would like to meet you also."

Emma wanted to go, but she could not accept without her stepmother's approval.

"We will be delighted to visit you, Mr. Fairchild. It is so thoughtful of you to invite us. And I'm sure it will be the first of many visits for us . . . or rather for me!" the woman tittered. "Emma, of course, will be at home there. But I'm sure she will need her mother with her often for guidance."

Not if I have anything to say about it, Mr. Fairchild promised himself. The woman irritated him. Thank goodness his wife was not the woman's actual daughter. Good manners forced him to extend his invitation to Mr. Chadwell also, but he silently gave thanks when it was rejected.

"Thank you, but I have other business at hand. You may soon be able to wish me joy as well, Mr. Fairchild."

"Oh? That will be my pleasure, Chadwell."

"Yes. I've found me a plump little heiress. Ten thousand pounds a year. Any man would get leg-shackled for that amount, right, Fairchild?"

Mr. Fairchild stared coldly at the youth while he silently pitied whatever young woman he had caught in his trap. He looked at Emma to discover her reaction to such callous talk, but she had hidden her eyes once more.

"I wonder, Miss Chadwell, if you would care for a drive in the park? Since your cold seems to be dissipating, you might enjoy some fresh air." He waited hopefully for her answer.

Instead, Mrs. Chadwell responded. "Now, now, Mr. Fairchild, you must not become too eager. She must stay in to overcome her cold if she is to accompany you to the country. You'll see enough of her once the knot is tied."

The woman's archness grated on his nerves. "Surely she will be recovered by our departure. Have you had a doctor to call?"

"No, we have not called a doctor, but it is not necessary. She will be recovered in a couple of more days. I, of course, must busy myself with the packing to be done if we are to be ready to leave for Fairchild House on . . . What day are we leaving, Mr. Fairchild?" Mrs. Chadwell asked.

"Tuesday next, ma'am."

"Which reminds me, Fairchild," Charlie broke in. "I came here on purpose this morning to settle on a wedding date. Now that Emma is getting back in her usual frame, it seems to me there is no reason to put it off."

"What did you have in mind, Chadwell? I'm afraid we cannot be married before the bans have been called."

"No, no, of course not. Didn't mean there was any big hurry. I mean, m'sister's not increasing, or anything like that!" the man hurriedly assured him, causing a stark protest from his mother and a gasp from Emma. "I just meant . . . well, you know, best to get it over with so the girl won't get too nervous, you know."

Or so you can collect the full settlement and pay off your pressing debts, Mr. Fairchild thought cynically. He made no response, waiting for the man's next move.

"Well, what I mean is, no need for a lot of fancy clothes. Won't take long for a wedding dress. She might even have something in her wardrobe that will do. No sense in spending more on her. Had to buy a whole new wardrobe for her visit to London."

"I think it would be best if we consulted my mother when we arrive at my estate. After all, your mother will be there and the two of them can discuss it at length. Mothers enjoy that sort of thing, you know," Mr. Fairchild said smoothly.

"Oh . . . uh, guess you are right, but . . . right, the ladies will decide," the young man said after a glare from his mother.

"Now, since I am to be denied Miss Chadwell's company on my morning drive, I had best be off. My horses do not stand well. I will send word of the time of our departure, and, of course, will put my travelling carriage at your disposal, Mrs. Chadwell." With a smile, he rose to his feet and gave a slight bow and departed.

Emma was allowed to return to her room after Mr. Fairchild's visit. She had spent most of her days there since her brother had informed her of Mr. Fairchild's offer. Nancy, her loyal maid, had nursed her cold, bringing up new remedies provided by Cook each day. Since her family left her alone most of the time, unwilling to risk infection, Emma had a lot of time to think.

She really was not against the marriage any longer. She had lived in a dream world, thinking she could remain at home and nothing would change. Now she forced herself to face reality. With her brother's marriage, there would be no place for her except that of an old maid, a poor relative with nothing to call her own. Life as the wife of a respected member of the *ton*, who could afford whatever she desired, was much to be preferred. Until today, it had seemed a cold, sterile choice. But now, she knew, there was a child.

The child. That had been a surprise. It took her mind from her mourning of her past life and her apprehension of the future. A motherless girl would give meaning to her days. Four years old would be about the age of Cook's grandchild back home. Perhaps she would even call her Mama. For the first time in a wretched week, Emma thought to the future with some pleasure.

Mr. Fairchild seemed to like town life. He'd never mentioned his estate. Perhaps he would even return to town at frequent intervals, leaving her in the country to be with the child and enjoy the kind of life she had always preferred.

Emma was already standing by the window of her bedroom when Nancy came in to awaken her on the day of their journey. She walked over to the still figure and placed both arms around her.

"Don't worry, love. This Mr. Fairchild seems to be a nice man."

"Of course, but . . . I thought it would be so simple. I would attend a few parties and then I could go home and everything would be as before. But it did not happen that way. Now I will never be able to return home again."

"Nothing in this life is simple, child, and it could've turned out worse than this."

"Yes, of course. Well," Emma said briskly, stepping out of the maid's arms. "What frightful horror am I to wear today?"

Nancy's mouth turned down. "The worst. That dark orange travelling dress."

Emma shuddered. The gown had ruffles, even though it was a travelling costume, and also large black buttons, with horse heads carved on them, down the front of it. The colour made her look quite ill. She hated the thought of meeting her mother-in-law-elect . . . how strange that sounded . . . and Mr. Fairchild's little daughter in that gown. But in spite of the freedom her engagement gave her, she was forced to continue wearing the same unsuitable gowns. There were no funds for more clothes, even if she could have convinced her stepmother and stepbrother of her need. But at least she was allowed to keep her hair in its simple style.

When she descended to the first floor, her stepmother greeted her with no demur other than a general reference to her lack of beauty. But Emma was used to that. Whatever else her stepmother might have said was cut off by the sound of a carriage arriving.

"Exactly on time. Remember that, my love. Your future husband appreciates promptness. When one's servants are prompt, that means the master demands it."

"Yes, Mama."

"How nice that we shall be travelling in such luxury, for I am sure Mr. Fairchild's travelling carriage is luxurious. Our carriage is a shambles. I did tell you he invited Mrs. Harris and her daughter, Deborah, did I not?"

"Yes, Mama."

"Well, you be sure and don't let that young lady upstage you. After all, you are the one Mr. Fairchild chose, even if she is prettier!"

A rapping at the door caused Mrs. Chadwell to halt her orders and turn with a pleasant smile pasted on her face. It disappeared, however, when the butler admitted a liveried servant. Before the servant could speak, Mrs. Chadwell demanded, "Where is Mr. Fairchild?"

The servant, an older man of pleasant mien, smiled at the sharp question and replied, "Mr. Fairchild and Lord Atherton have gone on ahead to arrange refreshments for you later, madam. My name is Adams, at your service," he said with a small bow. "Mr. Fairchild, my master, asked me to ensure your comfort on the journey."

The man's gracious dignity did much to soothe Mrs. Chadwell. "Well, I suppose that will be all right. Are the Harrises meeting us at whatever inn we will be stopping at?"

Adams looked surprised but swiftly recovered before Mrs. Chadwell noticed. "I beg your pardon, Mrs. Chadwell. I thought Mr. Fairchild would have informed you. Mrs. Harris and her daughter are travelling in the carriage with you. Mr. Fairchild thought you might enjoy the company on the journey."

"That is impossible!" Mrs. Chadwell snapped. "We are each taking a maid. There will not be room!"

"There is a second carriage for the servants, Mrs. Chadwell. Mr. Fairchild would not expect you to travel in the same carriage as your servants."

Emma hid a smile at the man's skill. He made his employer's arrangements appear a compliment to her mother, making it impossible for her to reject them.

"Oh! Well, of course, how thoughtful of Mr. Fairchild. Shall we go, then? We, of course, are ready. We would not be so unmannerly as to keep Mr. Fairchild's horses standing."

Emma groaned silently. If her stepmother was so intent on vaunting her every virtue, and even a few of Emma's, could she find any, it would be a highly embarrassing trip.

Mrs. Harris and her daughter were also ready and waiting when the carriage arrived at their house. Adams was gone only a few moments before the carriage door was swung open and Mrs. Harris and Deborah were handed in.

Mrs. Chadwell had made sure she and her stepdaughter sat facing the horses. However, when Mrs. Harris entered the carriage, Emma said quietly, "I do not mind riding with my back to the horses if it disturbs you, Mrs. Harris."

Katherine Harris was surprised and pleased at such consideration. She had had almost no contact with Miss Chadwell, but what she knew of the mother had not foreboded a pleasant visit. Now she smiled warmly at the poorly dressed young woman. "Why, thank you, Miss Chadwell. I will admit it does make me queasy."

"Emma! You should not . . . well, of course, that will be just fine," Mrs. Chadwell agreed huffily as Emma moved across the carriage. "Sometimes one's children can be such a disappointment to a mother. Don't you find that is true, Mrs. Harris?"

The woman smiled warmly at her daughter, a blue-eyed brunette beauty, before answering. "No, Mrs. Chadwell, on the whole, I cannot imagine a better life without my Deborah."

"Oh, Mama!" Deborah protested as she blushed and laughed.

Emma admired the young woman's prettiness, but even more admirable was the love between parent and child. It reminded her a little of the closeness she had shared with her father, and brought a welling of loneliness that caused her to turn and stare out the window.

"Well, some children are more pleasurable than others. My Aurora, Emma's stepsister, was a joy to behold. Everything looked absolutely beautiful on her, and all the men flocked around her. Why, it was more than I could do to keep up with all their names. And the house was constantly flooded with flowers that arrived each day. My little Aurora would just laugh and enslave more men the next evening. What a delightful . . ."

Before Mrs. Chadwell paused to take a breath, she had lost her audience. Emma, long used to unending commendations of her stepsister, continued to stare at the streets of London that grew less and less crowded as they reached the outskirts of the great city.

Deborah opened a book. Mrs. Harris, to whom most of Mrs. Chadwell's comments were addressed, was forced to remain at attention, but her eyes glazed over and her mind dealt with several ideas for retaliation on Mr. Fairchild for placing her beside this woman for a six-hour carriage ride.

When the carriage pulled into the yard of a prosperous inn only several hours' drive from Fairchild House, Mrs. Harris had a pounding headache and Mrs. Chadwell had finally run out of things to praise in her daughter. Emma was looking for a chance to stretch her legs, and Deborah was craning her neck in an unladylike manner, as her mother informed her, to determine whether Lord Atherton and Mr. Fairchild were awaiting their arrival.

As Adams swung open the carriage door, Mr. Fairchild, followed reluctantly by Lord Atherton, came from inside the inn to greet the travellers.

"Good afternoon, ladies. I trust Adams took good care of you?"

There were general murmurs of approbation of Adams's work, but Mr. Fairchild was surprised to receive a murderous glare from Mrs. Harris. Though his eyebrows rose, he said nothing, only escorting them all into the inn. "I have reserved a bedchamber for your convenience, and when you are ready, a luncheon will be laid out in a private parlour."

All four ladies ascended the stairs to refresh themselves before they sat down to luncheon. When Mrs. Harris was sure Mrs. Chadwell was going to eat, she said quietly, "I find I have a slight headache. I believe I will just lie down here and rest while you eat."

Mrs. Chadwell took no notice other than to assure the pale woman that she and her stepdaughter enjoyed perfect health. Then she sailed from the room, calling Emma to follow. Deborah, knowing her mother seldom suffered from headaches, helped her to lie down, but it was Emma who prepared a wet cloth to place on her forehead.

Again Mrs. Harris was surprised, but she was grateful. The cloth was soothing to her throbbing temples. The two young ladies descended the stairs, for the first time speaking to each other.

"Thank you for thinking of the cloth, Miss Chadwell. Mama does not often suffer from headaches."

"It is all right, Miss Harris. My stepmother's conversation has that effect on many people."

Deborah glanced swiftly at Emma's face, but she could

detect no laugh to accompany her remark. Not knowing how to respond, Deborah followed her into the parlour.

Emma spoke to Mr. Fairchild as he seated her at the table, asking that a pot of tea and a light luncheon be taken up to Mrs. Harris. Mr. Fairchild was also surprised at Miss Chadwell's consideration. It was another sign, albeit a small one, that he had chosen his future wife wisely.

During the final stage of the journey, Emma explained to her mother that it would be best if they did not talk during the drive because of Mrs. Harris's headache. Though Mrs. Chadwell sniffed at such sickliness, she complied, eventually falling asleep.

Even though Mrs. Harris had to tolerate slight snores that punctuated the air, it was more bearable than the woman's insufferable chatter. The result was the disappearance of her headache by the time the carriage turned into the long drive leading up to Fairchild House.

When she realised they were almost to their destination, Emma clenched her hands nervously. Mrs. Harris, seeing her alarm, reached over to pat her gently on her hands. "You will like Mrs. Fairchild. She is a wonderful lady."

Emma tried to smile in return, but her lips quivered and she quickly pressed them together. "Have you met Mr. Fairchild's daughter?"

"Yes, but only once. When we went to London for the beginning of this year's Season, we stopped to visit with Mrs. Fairchild for a few days. We are old friends, you see. And I saw the child several times then. She is beautiful, but Elaine is spoiling her. It is difficult to raise an only child."

"I suppose—"

"What? What? Are we there?" Mrs. Chadwell gasped, sitting upright suddenly.

"We are approaching Fairchild House now, Mrs. Chadwell," Mrs. Harris said.

"Well, that was not such a difficult journey, was it, my love? I'll be able to come down whenever you have need of me once you are married," Mrs. Chadwell assured her stepdaughter in a self-satisfied manner.

"Yes, Mama."

= 6 =

EMMA WAS THE LAST of the four women to enter the sunlit parlour to which the butler showed them. She nervously regarded the woman seated on the sofa, calmly plying her needle. Though her face showed her age, she stood with youthful agility, and her dark hair showed only a smattering of grey.

Mrs. Fairchild greeted the Harrises warmly and turned to Emma and her stepmother. With a sinking of her heart, Emma knew she would not show to advantage next to Deborah's petite prettiness.

Mr. Fairchild stepped forward to kiss his mother on the cheek. "Mother, may I present Mrs. Chadwell and her daughter, Miss Chadwell."

"Good afternoon, Mrs. Chadwell. Welcome to Fairchild House. And I am so pleased to meet you, Miss Chadwell."

Before Emma could respond, her stepmother stepped forward. "Yes, thank you, it is a lovely house, quite large. I'm sure Emma will be able to manage it just fine. All my children have been taught the necessary skills to manage a household, of course."

Emma's eyes closed in momentary embarrassment before she quietly thanked her hostess. At least her future mother-in-law was not a petite doll. That kind of woman always made Emma feel overlarge and awkward.

"Won't you be seated? I have sent for the tea tray. I expect you would like something to drink before being shown to your rooms. Katherine, how nice to see you again. And Deborah, you are looking in fine form. London Society must be agreeing with you."

"Yes, thank you, ma'am," Deborah replied with a blush while the two women embraced.

When all were seated, with the two men joining the ladies, the butler entered, followed by several footmen carrying a generous repast.

As she poured out, Mrs. Fairchild said, "Then you have a large family, Mrs. Chadwell?"

"I have three precious children, Mrs. Fairchild. Emma, of course, is my stepdaughter, but I have had the raising of her since she was two. My son, Charlie, is quite a fashionable young man, and my daughter, Aurora, made her debut several years ago. She was the most beautiful young lady presented that year and had her choice of all the young men. It is too bad Mr. Fairchild was not seeking a bride that year, or he would surely have chosen Aurora."

Emma's cheeks flooded with shame as Mrs. Fairchild struggled to find a response. "But . . . but of course you are pleased he has chosen Miss Chadwell."

"Well, I guess she'll have to do," Mrs. Chadwell said with a giggle, "because my beautiful Aurora was snatched up."

"Yes, well, Miss Chadwell, do you enjoy the country?"

Not allowing Emma to speak, Mrs. Chadwell answered for her. "Oh, my, yes, that's Emma. She's much happier in the country than the city. She doesn't feel as awkward as she does in the city. She's so tall, you know."

Emma sank down in her chair.

"If you are all ready, I'll have the housekeeper show you to your rooms," Mrs. Fairchild offered, a harried expression on her face. Since there was no demur, she rang for her housekeeper, Mrs. Quigley. As the party followed the housekeeper from the room, Mrs. Fairchild held back her son.

When the door closed behind the others, Mr. Fairchild turned to face his mother. "Well, Mother, what do you think?"

His mother's response was cautious. "I find Miss Chadwell an . . . interesting young woman. How long have you known her?"

"Approximately two weeks."

"But you felt you knew her well enough to risk . . . to ask her to marry you?"

"I do not need to know her, Mother. I'm marrying for you and Melissa."

"I beg your pardon?"

"I know you are lonely stuck down here in the country, and raising Melissa is no easy task. I thought if I provided a mother for the child, it would relieve you of some of the responsibility as well as provide you company."

"I have never asked for such a sacrifice from you, Richard, and I hardly think those appropriate reasons for marriage."

His sardonic expression underscored his words. "Those are the only reasons I would ever consider marriage, Mother. I tried marrying for love, remember?"

"Oh! That was not love. That was infatuation! And it does not mean you must discover the exact opposite of Diana in every respect. That poor child . . . I mean, Miss Chadwell is . . . she does not seem comfortable around strangers. I suppose this is an awkward meeting for her."

"She improves away from her stepmother."

"Anyone would," Mrs. Fairchild muttered. "Well, I am looking forward to becoming better acquainted. Do you want me to have a soirée to introduce her to the neighbours?"

"No, there will be time enough for that after the wedding. However, if Miss Chadwell has no objection, I would like to be married from here."

"Have you discussed the wedding with her?"

"No," Mr. Fairchild said, weariness showing in his voice. "Only with her brother, who, fortunately, couldn't join us."

"Oh. Well, I must go check with Mrs. Quigley to see if there are any problems. Melissa is in the nursery if you would care to say hello to her."

"I doubt she would be interested in seeing me."

Emma was not overly tired from the journey. After changing from the hated travelling gown to the dinner gown her mother had planned for her to wear, Emma left her well-proportioned, pleasant room.

In the hallway, she stopped a young maid and asked if Miss Fairchild was in the nursery and could she direct her there. Though she appeared surprised by the guest's request, the maid gave her the information she sought and scurried away.

Emma knew her behaviour was not exactly what it should be, but she was so anxious to see the child, she was willing to risk Mr. Fairchild's displeasure. She slipped up the back stairs and found the third door on the left, just as the maid had said, and rapped softly.

Another young maid opened the door and Emma explained that she was a visitor and would like to meet Miss Fairchild. The maid backed away from the door, allowing Emma to enter, and for the first time Emma saw the pretty blond child who was to become her daughter.

"Hello, my name is Miss Chadwell, and I wanted to meet you."

The child looked up at Emma with big blue eyes and studied her solemnly. "Hello," she finally said.

"What is your name?"

" 'Lissa," the child said clearly before turning her attention back to the rag doll she was holding.

"Her name's Miss Melissa, ma'am."

"Do you mind if I sit down and talk to you, Melissa?" Emma asked gently, already enthralled with the child. When there was no objection from the small girl, she sat beside her and chatted with her about her dolly.

"I do not understand where Emma could be. She is always very prompt, I assure you, Mr. Fairchild. I stopped by her room to be sure she . . . that is, to accompany her down. But since she was not there, I assumed she had already descended. I wonder if you should send someone to search for her, Mr. Fairchild. After all, this is a large house. Not that Emma is not used to large houses," Mrs. Chadwell assured everyone in a loud voice. Dinner had not even begun, and already Mrs. Chadwell was exhausting the company.

The door opened in the middle of her complaint, and a rather flustered Emma slipped into the room. "I'm sorry," was as much as the young woman managed to say before her stepmother descended upon her.

"Emma, where have you been? I looked for you in your room and I thought you would be down here, but when I arrived, you were not here. Just where were you, and you be sure you apologise to Mr. Fairchild for your tardiness. After all, I just assured him you were always on time. You are such a disappointment to me sometimes. I cannot—"

Mr. Fairchild interrupted. "Miss Chadwell has apologised, Mrs. Chadwell. I see no need for such a fuss. Shall we go in to dinner?" he suggested.

The company moved en masse toward the door, hoping to escape Mrs. Chadwell. However, order was restored by Mrs. Fairchild. "Richard, please escort Mrs. Chadwell to dinner, and Lord Atherton, if you will take in Mrs. Harris, the young ladies and I will follow."

Mrs. Fairchild ignored her son's displeasure. He had brought the woman upon them. It was only fair that he bear the burden of entertaining her. And at least going in to dinner stopped the woman from berating that poor child. She felt sorry for Miss Chadwell. She wasn't sure the girl would be the perfect wife for her son, but she certainly could be charitable, considering the cross the child had to bear.

Once seated around the table, the others were pleased to discover that Mrs. Chadwell took eating seriously and did not spend much time on dinner conversation. Lord Atherton, who was seated between the two older women, was relieved to find he need converse with only Mrs. Harris. In addition, Miss Harris was seated across from him, and his eyes frequently fell on her. She was a fetching little thing, all rosy cheeks and laughing eyes, her dark curls framing a pretty face.

Mrs. Harris, noting Lord Atherton's preoccupation with her daughter, could not help but be pleased. She turned to talk to Elaine Fairchild and found a smile and a questioning look on her face.

"I do not know," Mrs. Harris said quietly. "I believe she is interested, but time will tell."

"That would be lovely, Katherine. We shall see what we can do to help things along. But what about the Chadwells? Do you know anything about them?"

Mrs. Harris hesitated. "Well, as you can imagine, Mrs. Chadwell is not well liked. The girl says almost nothing in public. She has had little success during the Season. I admit to being surprised when I read the announcement in the papers."

"I believe he is choosing the most opposite of women from Diana. She disillusioned him."

"Perhaps this marriage will prove happy. She seems a kind and considerate girl," Mrs. Harris said, remembering Emma's kindness on the journey.

"We shall see. I will admit I am not too happy about it. Oh, I want Richard to remarry, but . . . but surely there is someone a little more lively who could arouse his emotions."

Mrs. Fairchild rose from her bed in a thoughtful frame of mind. The previous evening had been a disaster. Mrs. Chadwell had dominated the conversation after dinner. Mrs. Fairchild had had no opportunity to talk to Katherine Harris or get to know Miss Chadwell. The few times she had managed to ask Miss Chadwell any questions, her stepmother had answered for her.

And if her son thought he was going to enjoy his evenings in the billiard room, leaving her to endure Mrs. Chadwell, he was quite mistaken. That would be settled this morning!

It was also time he greet his daughter. It was bad enough that he spent so little time with her, but to ignore her completely would harm the child.

After she was dressed with her usual quiet style, Mrs. Fairchild ascended the stairs to see Melissa before going down to begin her day in the breakfast parlour. When she reached the third floor, the stillness of the morning was broken by a tinkling laugh, not heard often enough as far as Mrs. Fairchild was concerned. She wondered what could be giving Melissa such pleasure so early in the morning.

Swinging open the door to the nursery, she was startled to see Miss Chadwell holding Melissa in her lap, seated by the window. Her sweet voice was speaking quietly to the child, and she held a piece of paper and charcoal in her hands. Even as Mrs. Fairchild watched, the swiftly moving fingers sketched something on the paper that again brought laughter to the little girl.

"Good morning," Mrs. Fairchild said, watching for the young woman's reaction.

"Oh! Oh, good morning, Mrs. Fairchild. I hope you do not mind but . . ."

"Grandmama," the child exclaimed, slipping off the comfortable lap and running to her grandmother, "come see what Miss Emma can draw!"

"Miss Emma?"

Embarrassed, Emma rose. "I asked her to call me that, Mrs. Fairchild. Miss Chadwell seemed so formal."

"If that is what you prefer, my dear, of course she may do so." Mrs. Fairchild studied the young woman. She might not be a beauty, though her appearance was much improved by the plain blue gown she wore, but Mrs. Fairchild was much more receptive to her as her daughter-in-law now. She had won her over by her interest in Melissa. "I did not know you had met my granddaughter."

"I know I should have waited for you or . . . or Mr. Fairchild to introduce us, but I was anxious to meet her. So yesterday, after our arrival, I asked one of the maids to direct me and . . . and I visited Melissa. She was very gracious and asked me to come again," Emma finished, with a warm smile to the child that lit up her entire face.

Why, she's attractive when she smiles like that, Mrs. Fairchild thought before she was distracted by the child's tuggings on her hand. "Come see, Grandmama."

"Yes, of course, child," she agreed, though her mind was sifting through this new image of her future daughter-in-law. When she saw the drawing Melissa showed her as proudly as if she had done it herself, Mrs. Fairchild forgot her thoughts. "Why, that's very good. You certainly have a talent for humourous drawings, Miss Chadwell."

Emma, used to having her drawings dismissed by her family because they were not the watercolours produced by Aurora, said, "Thank you, ma'am, but they are just sketches to go with the story I was telling Melissa."

"It was funny, Grandmama. The maid spilled all the milk and the butler fell down because it was slippery and the master didn't have any milk for his breakfast. That's 'cause he didn't like milk, but when he couldn't have any, he liked it! Miss Emma says I should drink my milk 'cause it makes me strong."

"Miss Emma is correct," Mrs. Fairchild said, smiling ruefully. To Emma she said, "I've been forcing milk on this child for a long time. I'm glad you found a way for her to enjoy it."

"My father had a great interest in science, and he believed it was important for our nourishment."

"Oh, really? How interesting. You must tell me more about his theories."

Normally, Emma was shy about talking to strangers, but the topic of her father loosened her tongue. The three of them sat down at a table where Melissa could finish her milk, only occasionally insisting on another drawing to keep her interested, and Mrs. Fairchild and Emma talked about her father and the theories he had expounded to his daughter.

After an hour with Miss Chadwell, one that Mrs. Fairchild found informative in more than scientific theories, she said regretfully that they would need to descend for breakfast. Melissa reacted in the manner that had become more and more frequent the past few months—screaming and protesting whenever something displeased her.

Emma looked hesitantly at Mrs. Fairchild. When she received a nod from that lady, she took matters in her own hands. Taking the child by both shoulders, she shook her lightly, shocking her.

"Melissa, listen to me. If you would like me to come visit you again, I will be glad to do so. But I will not come visit a child who acts like this. Do you want me to come visit you again?"

Big blue eyes with tears hovering on the edges looked up at Emma, almost causing her to give in before she accomplished her goal. But she remained firm, and Melissa gave a troubled nod.

"Good. I hoped you would want me to come back, because I truly enjoyed seeing you. Perhaps, if your grandmama does not object, we could go for a walk this afternoon and you could show me the pretty flowers in the garden."

"Oh, please, Grandmama, please?"

"Yes, of course, if Miss Chadwell wants to."

"Then I will see you this afternoon after you rest. You do lie down each afternoon, don't you?"

The child gave a doubtful look at both adults before saying slowly, "I will today if you want me to."

"I do, Melissa. May I give you a hug before I leave?"

The little girl cast herself into Emma's outstretched arms and then, with a little encouragement from Emma, gave her grandmother a hug also.

Out in the hallway, after the maid had been called to keep an eye on Melissa, Mrs. Fairchild held out her hand to Miss Chadwell. "My dear, that was marvellous. Have you known many children?"

"Just those on the estate, ma'am. I relied on my instincts. I hope you didn't mind my directing her behaviour as I did?"

"No, my dear, I was delighted. As you are going to be her new mama, it will be up to you to manage her. And I believe you are going to be a wonderful mother. I am so pleased."

"Thank you, ma'am. I am delighted to have Melissa. I love children."

"Come, let's go down to breakfast. Uh . . . does your mother usually come down to breakfast, or would she prefer a tray in her room?"

"At home, she usually has a tray, ma'am, but I do not know what she would prefer here."

"Ah. Well, if she has not arrived at the breakfast table before us, I will send a tray up and see if that pleases her."

"That is most kind of you, Mrs. Fairchild. I will join you as soon as I change."

"Change? But that dress is acceptable for breakfast."

"Thank you, but Mama has already chosen what she would like for me to wear."

"Nonsense. I will explain to your mother that I thought

you charming as you are now and would not allow fashion to delay breakfast."

Though Emma knew she risked her stepmother's displeasure, an unpleasant occurrence, she wanted to please Mrs. Fairchild. With a smile, she accompanied that determined lady downstairs to the breakfast parlour.

The two ladies discovered everyone before them except Mrs. Chadwell. Mrs. Fairchild hastily asked Mrs. Quigley to send a tray to her room, hoping to avoid her company for at least a while.

As Mrs. Quigley served the newcomers, Mrs. Harris leaned forward to say, "Elaine, I came to your room this morning, but you were not there."

"Oh, we—I was visiting with Melissa." Mrs. Fairchild sent an apologetic smile to Emma, whose face expressed her unease.

"Ah. How is the child?"

"Delightful."

"Really, Mother, Mrs. Harris is a friend," Mr. Fairchild intervened from the opposite end of the small table. "There is no need to tell lies."

Emma looked at her future husband in shock. She had had no idea the man did not care for his child. His gaze met hers, and she saw no regret for his harsh words.

"How would you know it is a lie?" Mrs. Fairchild challenged. "I doubt that you have seen your daughter for longer than a quarter hour in the entire past year."

Mr. Fairchild pressed his lips firmly together and rearranged his silverware before changing the subject. "Have you seen Mrs. Chadwell this morning?"

Emma kept her gaze fixed on her plate, and Mrs. Fairchild answered. "Emma says she prefers a tray in her room, and I asked Quigley to send one up to her."

"Then we will not wait any longer," he said, pushing back his chair. His mother's raised eyebrows brought an explanation. "I am going to show Lord Atherton that new colt Peters is training for me."

"I believe Emma and Deborah might enjoy such an outing, if, of course, you can spare the time for them to finish their breakfasts," Mrs. Fairchild responded. Her pointed reminder of his duties as host brought a flush to Mr. Fairchild's face.

Lord Atherton appeared startled as well. He looked across the table at Miss Harris in surprise, and Emma bit back a smile.

Her eyes travelled on to Mr. Fairchild to discover irritation as his gaze met hers. In the face of his mother's instructions, however, he had no choice but to extend the invitation. Emma, eager to be out and about, set aside her misgivings about her welcome and accepted with a smile.

Deborah smiled shyly at Lord Atherton as she said, "I would love to look at the horses if the gentlemen do not mind."

Both men assured her of their delight, but Emma did not mistake the grimace on Mr. Fairchild's face as a smile of pleasure. He clearly did not look forward to time spent in her company. She had no large dowry, and she was no beauty. Exactly why had he proposed to her?

"Wonderful," Mrs. Fairchild said when all was arranged, "and Richard, since you have already finished your breakfast, perhaps I might have a word with you privately while the others enjoy their meal."

= 7 =

GOOD MANNERS FORCED Mr. Fairchild to accede to his mother's request, and he rose and escorted her from the dining hall to the morning room, her preference for conducting the household chores.

"Well, Mother, what are you going to rake me over the coals for?"

Mrs. Fairchild took a deep breath, irritated that her son would tease her out of her anger. "What makes you think I want to rake you over the coals?"

Richard Fairchild smiled grimly. "It is not so long since I have displeased you as a young man to recognise the signs."

"All right, perhaps I am a little displeased with your behaviour. But, as your mother . . ."

"You have every right to berate me."

His warm smile disarmed her, as he intended it should. "Oh, Richard! Son, I do love you, but if you and Lord Atherton abandon us ladies to Mrs. Chadwell again and depart merrily for the billiard room, I swear I will disown you! The woman is enough to try a saint, and, after all, it is your fault she is here."

"You are right, Mother," Mr. Fairchild agreed with a rueful laugh. "I took the cowardly way out. I promise not to do so again. Anything else?"

Mrs. Fairchild rose and walked away from her son.

"Ah, I see the topic is the perennial one of my daughter. What is it now, Mother?"

"Richard, I have tried to be understanding, but . . . but ignoring Melissa's existence is not the answer."

"I am not ignoring her, Mother. I am sacrificing my free-dom—and probably my happiness—for the child's sake, so that she will have a mother."

"What about a father? Does the child not deserve a father?"

"I am her father, but that does not mean that I must spend every waking moment of my time with her." He sighed and rubbed the back of his neck. They had had this argument before.

"No, but I do believe it means you should at least see her when you return home at long last."

It was Mr. Fairchild's turn to pace. Finally, he swung around to face the anxious woman. "Yes, of course, you are right, Mother, as usual. I will go see Melissa this afternoon. And I suppose I must present her to Miss Chadwell as well. I have been postponing their introduction because I am afraid the young woman will take one look and break our engagement. Then it would be all to do over again."

"I doubt that Emma will behave in that way," Mrs. Fair-child said, avoiding her son's gaze.

"You must have gotten to know Miss Chadwell quite well last evening to be calling her by her first name."

"We have spent some time talking."

"And are you opposed to our engagement?" Mr. Fairchild asked curiously, having expected more protests from his mother.

"No, I don't believe I am. In fact, I think you may have chosen more wisely than you realise. I have decided I should congratulate you on your discernment instead."

Mr. Fairchild frowned as he considered her words.

"Do you have an interest in horses, Miss Chadwell, or did you simply want to enjoy the fresh air?" Mr. Fairchild asked, hoping to evoke some response from the young lady accompanying him. She had not spoken a word since he rejoined the others.

Emma, who had been enjoying the scent of spring, was startled by his sudden question. "Oh! I . . . both, Mr. Fairchild."

"Ah, that is a diplomatic answer. Well, I will try not to

bore you overlong with the horses. Lord Atherton and I can return at a later date when you are otherwise occupied."

Emma wanted to protest that she loved horses and was quite knowledgeable about them, but she kept silent.

"Would you care to meet my daughter this afternoon? I have not yet visited her, but I feel sure she will be available if it is convenient to you."

"Well . . . the truth is I've already met your daughter."

Mr. Fairchild stared at the embarrassed young woman, then his eyes narrowed. "My mother did not mention that."

"You must not—"

"Never mind. Since you have met my daughter, I suppose you are not desirous of spending more time with her."

"Mr. Fairchild! How can you say such a thing? I have already made plans with Melissa for a walk this afternoon. You may join us if you would like."

Miss Chadwell sounded a little like his mother, and Mr. Fairchild bit back a smile. Now he understood his mother's congratulations. "Thank you. That would be most enjoyable."

Since they had reached the stables, Mr. Fairchild included the other two in their conversation as he talked about the horses. Emma noted the ease with which Deborah carried on a conversation with Lord Atherton and even Mr. Fairchild.

Lord Atherton appeared equally impressed. After some minutes, he asked, "Miss Harris, are you truly interested in horses?"

The young lady's cheeks burned brightly as she confessed, "I don't know much about them, Lord Atherton, but I would like to learn."

Emma was surprised by the envy she felt at Lord Atherton's smile as he took Deborah's hand in his. "I will be pleased to teach you about horses, Miss Harris."

Had Mr. Fairchild been so besotted about his first wife as Lord Atherton was fast becoming over Miss Harris? That question occupied Emma's mind as much as the horses.

When they returned to the house, Lord Atherton's appreciation of Miss Harris's charms seemed to have grown. "Um . . . I believe I shall go to the billiard room, if any of you would care to join me?"

Emma smiled and nodded her head no, and Mr. Fairchild offered the excuse of paperwork, but Deborah stared at the gentleman wide-eyed. "I didn't know any ladies ever played that game. I would love to learn, Lord Atherton, if you would not mind."

Emma watched over her shoulder as the two hurried off to the game of billiards, their minds obviously on romance more than games. Mr. Fairchild, on the other hand, never looked back.

With a sigh, Emma continued up the stairs. She'd best change into the dress her mother selected for her before that lady discovered she had disobeyed her.

Luncheon was uneventful except for Mrs. Chadwell's presence. As on the night before, no general conversation was possible because the woman never stopped talking once her hunger was assuaged. Emma was embarrassed for her stepmother over and over again, which made it impossible for her to make any effort to converse.

After they left the table, Mr. Fairchild indicated he'd sent for Melissa to join them for a walk, and Emma joined father and daughter.

Melissa, after one look at her father, threw her arms around Emma. When her father reprimanded her for her manners, Emma remained frozen, unsure what was expected of her.

"No! I'se supposed to show Miss Emma the flowers. Not you!" the child screamed at her father.

Mr. Fairchild roared back, and the child fell into a tantrum before Emma could intervene. He shouted for the nursery maid, only halfway up the stairs, to return and take the heathen child back to the nursery.

"Mr. Fairchild! Surely you do not—"

"Enough, Miss Chadwell. I know how to deal with my child!"

Emma fell silent, but she did not agree with Mr. Fairchild. She considered his statement to be quite contrary to fact.

After Melissa's screams had faded, Mr. Fairchild turned to the silent woman beside him and said with clenched teeth, "Well, Miss Chadwell, now you see the problem. If you so desire, I will release you from your promise."

Emma stared at him uncomprehendingly until his words pierced her dazed brain. The irony almost caused her to break out in hysterical laughter. When she pleaded with him to leave her alone, he had refused. Now that she had no choice, he offered to release her. "No, I . . . she is not . . . I cannot." With those few phrases, Emma turned to flee up the stairs.

"Women!" Mr. Fairchild stormed, and headed for the male stronghold of the stable.

After another excruciatingly painful dinner, everyone adjourned to the parlour. The frown on Mr. Fairchild's face was pronounced, but he was remarkably patient with Mrs. Chadwell. He even offered a game of whist to her, enlisting Lord Atherton and Mrs. Harris.

Deborah excused herself to fetch some stitchery she was working on, and Mrs. Fairchild beckoned to Emma to join her in a private coze by the fire.

When Mrs. Fairchild asked about the outing with Melissa, all Emma could do was shake her head and fight to keep back the tears. She had been in despair all afternoon, thinking about Mr. Fairchild's words. She felt sure he regretted his offer, but she no longer wanted to return home. With her brother's approaching marriage, there was no place for her there. She felt adrift in a strange world.

"My dear, surely it could not've been that terrible," Mrs. Fairchild said kindly.

"Melissa and her father . . . they screamed at each other and she misbehaved very badly."

"But I felt sure you would be able to handle her!"

"I did not think it was my place to . . . Mr. Fairchild seemed . . ." Emma turned her face away.

"Oh, dear."

Emma sank her teeth into her bottom lip. Finally, she looked at the older woman. "It is almost as if he hates her." When Mrs. Fairchild said nothing, she asked, "Is it true?"

Mrs. Fairchild appeared to be choosing her words carefully as she attempted to answer Emma's question. "I truly don't think he hates her, but—but she reminds him of his wife—his first wife. Their marriage was a bitter disaster. He would never consider marriage again if it were not for the responsibility he feels to provide a mother for—" Realizing to whom she was speaking, Mrs. Fairchild broke off. "I am sorry, Emma."

"Is that why—" Emma stopped in embarrassment. "It is all right, ma'am," she assured the older woman. "I did wonder. I know I am not pretty or wealthy, and I did not expect—nor want—any offers."

"But if you dressed— Oh, dear, I seem to say everything I should not this evening."

Emma smiled and patted Mrs. Fairchild's clenched hands. "Don't concern yourself. I realise my wardrobe is . . ." She paused trying to find an appropriate word. With a laugh, she said, "Bizarre. But you see, I did not want—I hoped to return home and everything be like it was. But that's not possible."

"You mean you chose those strange gowns?"

"Oh, no, of course not. Mama chose my gowns, and, sadly enough, thinks them all the crack. I only chose not to argue with her. And now, when I would choose differently, there is no money left to purchase new gowns."

"It is of no matter since you are engaged to Richard," Mrs. Fairchild assured her. "Once you are married, Richard will provide you with a beautiful wardrobe. And I will love helping you choose it."

"Thank you, ma'am, but I think Mr. Fairchild is regretting his offer and . . . I believe I should release him," she admitted, her voice shaking.

"Don't you dare! You will be a wonderful mother for Melissa." She turned to glare at her son, who was entertaining Mrs. Chadwell.

Deborah joined them before Emma could protest, and the conversation changed to more general topics. Emma, however, brought the blood to Deborah's cheeks when she said, "Lord Atherton is an enjoyable companion. Has Mr. Fairchild known him long?"

Mrs. Fairchild looked at Deborah. "Ah, Emma has discovered a topic of conversation to your liking, Deborah?"

If anything, the girl's cheeks grew more red. Mrs. Fairchild chuckled. "Do not be embarrassed. You have chosen a fine man. And since Richard is going to marry, it would be nice for Lord Atherton to have a wife also."

A knock on the door followed by Quigley's entrance interrupted their conversation. Everyone but Mrs. Chadwell, who was concentrating on her cards, turned to watch as the butler came to Mr. Fairchild.

"An express just arrived from London for Mrs. Chadwell, sir."

"All right, Quigley," Mr. Fairchild said with a nod to the woman across from him.

"An express for me? It must be from my son, because Aurora is still visiting in Italy. Whatever could it be?" the woman said loudly, enjoying the importance she felt was attached to the receiving of such a message.

"We will leave you to read your message in peace," Mr. Fairchild assured her, relieved to have even a few minutes' break from the woman's incessant chatter. They had scarcely seated themselves, however, before Mrs. Chadwell, with a pleased exclamation, joined them.

"The most wonderful thing! This is from my son, Charlie. His suit has been accepted by Miss Mary Stokie, and they are to be married right away! He needs me in London to make arrangements for the festivities and to furbish up the town house. Oh, my, is this not exciting, Emma? We shall leave first thing in the morning. Oh, if that is all right with you, Mr. Fairchild. But, of course, you can see how I must return at once. A mother's place is with her child at a time like this."

With a look of relief that caused Emma's heart to sink even lower, Mr. Fairchild bowed to her stepmother. "Of course. I will be delighted to escort the two of you back to London."

Mrs. Fairchild hurriedly said, "Congratulations, Mrs. Chadwell. Soon all your children will be settled. But I wonder, if you do not have need of Emma, might she care to remain here with us until closer to the wedding? There is so much hustle and bustle surrounding a wedding, I fear she might grow fatigued before her own marriage."

Emma knew she should refuse the invitation. It was clear Mr. Fairchild would prefer her anywhere but at Fairchild House. But the thought of remaining here in the country, with pleasant companions and, she thought guiltily, away from her stepmother, was too tempting. If only her stepmother would permit it.

"Why, what a lovely invitation, Mrs. Fairchild. No, I have no need for Emma, and it would be fine for her to remain here in her future home for a few more days. Thank Mrs. Fairchild for her invitation, Emma."

Emma did so, but she avoided looking at her betrothed. She did not want to see the irritation she felt sure was there.

His stiff words could not be avoided. "I shall escort you to town tomorrow, Mrs. Chadwell, if you would like, to ensure your safe trip."

Ah. If she would not leave his presence, he would leave hers. Emma bowed her head and said nothing.

"Why, thank you, Mr. Fairchild. That is most considerate of you, though it really is not necessary."

"I also have some business to transact in London that recently came up. James, would you care to accompany me?"

"What?" said Lord Atherton, drawn away from the whispered conversation he was having with Miss Harris. "Oh, I don't think so, Richard, unless you have need of me. I will remain behind and lend the ladies my escort until you return."

"Very well, but I may have to stay a few days. Shall we make an early start, Mrs. Chadwell?"

"Certainly. I'll just go upstairs and start the maids packing. My, how exciting, Charlie getting married. Why, I haven't had such wonderful news since Aurora's engagement. My children bring me so much joy!" She rose and made her goodbyes, remembering Emma when she got to her. "Oh, Emma, I had almost forgotten you were here. Come with me, child. You may be able to help me organise the maids."

"Yes, Mama."

On a flow of chatter, Mrs. Chadwell and her daughter exited the room, leaving behind a relieved group of people.

"I know I should not say it, but I will be glad to see that woman leave," Mrs. Fairchild confessed.

"It would not have been a bad thing if both of them had departed," Mr. Fairchild said under his breath.

His mother frowned at him. "I hope you do not plan to stay long in London. Without her mother, Emma will feel much more comfortable and you will be able to get to know each other."

"We shall see, Mother."

When Emma entered the breakfast parlour the next morning, after her stepmother's early departure, Mrs. Fairchild looked up at her with a frown that startled the young woman.

"Good morning. Am I late?"

Immediately the frown was wiped away. "No, of course not, child. Quigley will bring a fresh pot of tea. I just wondered if you might not be more comfortable in a simpler gown . . . as you wore yesterday morning."

Emma looked down ruefully at the beruffled creation she was wearing. "Yes, I would, Mrs. Fairchild, but I'm afraid my wardrobe is limited, as I said last night."

"Hmmm," Mrs. Fairchild said, frowning again as she thought over the situation. "Ah! I have it. We are much the same height, though you are more slender than I. We'll have several of my gowns fitted to you."

"Oh, no! I could not let you do that."

"Nonsense, child. You cannot stop me. After breakfast, we will retire to my rooms and my maid will do the work. She'll have one ready for you this afternoon."

"But—"

"No protests, child. It will give me a lot of pleasure to see you at your best. Now, eat your breakfast and then we will have you transformed into the attractive young woman that is hiding beneath that hideous gown."

Emma followed her hostess's orders. It seemed she had

only changed one dictator for another, only this one's ideas of fashion coincided with her own.

Emma's first day at Fairchild House without her step-mother was enjoyable. Her opinion was sought and her wants attended to, and not once did anyone refer to her as a disappointment.

In addition, casual conversation was encouraged between Emma and Deborah. Though the other girl was younger, Emma found several things in common with Deborah, and it was her first experience of having a friend of equal social status. The servants at home had been close to her, but they had also looked to her for protection and guidance, a respon-sibility that she had willingly shouldered.

Emma blossomed in this relaxed atmosphere. There was laughter and lighthearted chatter, and in the days to follow, friendly excursions to the garden and even to a nearby ruined castle.

Melissa was invited to join them frequently, and Mrs. Fairchild encouraged Emma to guide the child in her be-haviour. Emma found great delight in the little girl and welcomed her presence whenever Melissa was able to ac-company her. This was a new experience for the child also, and she reveled in it. It did not take long for her to under-stand the rules Emma set out for her, and the pleasure of being with Miss Emma made them easy to follow.

Mrs. Fairchild watched the friendship grow between the young lady and her grandchild and gave thanks to God for her son's decision. But she grew more concerned each day as her son failed to put in an appearance. Lord Atherton, however, did not appear impatient with his friend's ab-sence. In fact, he seemed to be enjoying the carefree days, particularly since he spent them in Miss Harris's company.

When over a week had passed without Mr. Fairchild's re-turn, his mother decided it was time she did something about it. Sending the young people, along with Melissa, out for a picnic in a particularly pleasant meadow, she sat down and wrote a message to her son, telling Quigley to send it express.

"Will he not be . . . well, irritated by your letter?" Mrs. Harris asked hesitantly.

"Yes, of course he will," Elaine Fairchild agreed. "But he will not ignore it, either. I think it is time he got to know Emma better. She is perfect for him, Katherine, but I am afraid he will not realise that fact."

"It is hard to believe she is the same girl. She is attractive. Her eyes are lovely, and she has an almost willowy figure when she is properly dressed."

"Yes. But even more important, she loves Melissa and is good for her. The child's behaviour has improved a hundredfold since Emma's arrival."

"She is a darling child. She looks much like her mother, who was an acknowledged beauty."

"Yes, unfortunately she does. If she had looked more like her father, he might not associate her so much with his wife. By the time the woman died, they hated each other. Oh, Katherine, it was horrible. She was spoiled and spiteful. The few times I visited them, I never stayed longer than a few days because I could not stand their incessant fighting."

"But the child is not to blame for her mother's behaviour."

"And I have told Richard that many times, but when he looks at the child, he sees Diana. He cannot seem to control his reaction."

"Do you think when he returns he will realise how perfect Emma is?"

"I don't know," Mrs. Fairchild said, troubled by that thought. "I hope he will, but she . . . he had his choice of all the beauties in London. With his wealth, there is not a one of them who would turn him down."

"That is certainly true. In London, the women buzz around both him and Lord Atherton the moment they enter a ballroom."

"I know," Mrs. Fairchild said with a sigh. "But outward beauty does not guarantee happiness. As a matter of fact, those who are most celebrated for their outward beauty seem to have little beauty inside. Except Deborah, of course. She is a darling."

"Thank you," Mrs. Harris said with satisfaction. "Deborah is a good daughter . . . and I hope Lord Atherton appreciates her inner beauty."

Mrs. Fairchild chuckled. "Well, there is no doubt he appreciates her outer beauty."

"He does seem to be taken with her. But I am worried, Elaine. The child is head over heels, and if nothing comes of their time here together, she will be heartbroken."

"We will just pray that both men come to their senses and accept the bounty God has provided." With a sigh, she added, "And we must do all we can to help. I don't think Richard will receive the letter until this evening and . . . and he could arrive for dinner tomorrow evening. I will have Cook prepare his favourite dishes just in case. Do you know of any favourites of Lord Atherton?"

= 8 =

EMMA, DELIGHTING IN the days spent in the country, put off worry over Mr. Fairchild's feelings and set out to enjoy herself, an easy enough task with her companions. Melissa, however, after a week of joy, reminded her of her situation at breakfast one morning.

Escorted to the breakfast parlour by one of the maids as a special privilege, the child squealed, "Miss Emma, Miss Emma!" as soon as she saw her, twisting loose from the maid's hands and running to her.

"Melissa, that is not the way a lady enters the room," Emma reminded her sternly.

"Yes, but Miss Emma, guess what Meg said to Betty!"

Several pairs of eyes looked at the young maid who stood with her head down and her face an embarrassed pink. Emma turned back to the child. "Melissa, you are embarrassing Betty. You must beg her pardon."

Impatient with all these grown-up rules when she was about to burst with her news, Melissa whirled around to say, "Sorry, Betty" hurriedly before facing Emma again. "Can I tell you now?"

"Just a moment, Melissa," Mrs. Fairchild intervened. "You may go now, Betty."

"Thank you, ma'am . . . and . . . and we didn't mean no 'arm. Meg was just repeatin' what she 'eard in the kitchen."

"That is all right, child," Mrs. Fairchild assured the maid kindly. "You may go."

Betty hurried from the room before her employer changed her mind, and Emma turned to Melissa, hopping from one foot to the other. "What is it, love, that has you so excited."

"Oh, Miss Emma! Just wait until you hear. You are going to be my new mama! Isn't that wonderful?"

The child threw her little arms around Emma, and Emma involuntarily drew the child against her. She loved the warm feeling it gave her, but Emma was worried about what might happen when Mr. Fairchild returned. She met Mrs. Fairchild's eyes over the child and sent a plea for assistance.

"Melissa, Emma is not your mother yet, so you must just treat her as a good friend," Mrs. Fairchild said kindly. "But it is wonderful that she is going to be your mama," she added firmly, trying to convey her approval to the young woman holding her grandchild.

"And I may call you 'Mama'?" Melissa asked anxiously.

Emma could not resist the big blue eyes that watched her face so carefully. "Yes, darling, you may call me 'Mama'." After Melissa's excited squeal, Emma added, "But only after the . . . the ceremony."

"What ceremony?" the child demanded, impatient for her new mama.

Lord Atherton explained, "For Emma to become your mother, she must marry your father, Melissa."

"Why?" the child demanded, alarmed that the stern man who always made her cry had to be a part of the enchanted circle.

"Because he is your father, child," Mrs. Fairchild reminded her. "That is how Emma will become your mama."

"Do you mind, Miss Emma?" the child asked anxiously.

"No, sweetheart, I do not mind, but your father may— may find someone else he likes better. We shall just wait and see, okay?"

That thought caused Melissa's eyes to cloud over with tears, alarming Lord Atherton. "Here now, you mustn't cry. We are going to see that new pony Peters has found for you so you may start your riding lessons this morning. And you must first eat breakfast, young lady. Peters will not want you on his pony if you have not been properly fed yourself."

Emma added to Lord Atherton's distraction and convinced the child to eat her breakfast, putting aside any discussion of such a dangerous topic to another time. She didn't want to have to face that question any sooner than necessary. And she knew it would come soon enough.

Mrs. Fairchild and Mrs. Harris exchanged a look, both wondering if Mr. Fairchild would return that evening and what his reaction would be both to Emma and his child. Surely he could only approve of the changes in both, Mrs. Fairchild thought, if only he saw them at their best. But she feared Emma would become shy the moment he walked into the room. And there was no question but that Melissa did not care for her father.

With a sigh, Mrs. Fairchild continued with her breakfast. After all, she had done all she could until Richard returned. When that happened, it would be in God's hands. She just hoped He was paying attention.

Mr. Fairchild surprised his mother not only by heeding her summons, but also by appearing earlier than she thought possible. The three young people and Melissa had gone for another picnic when Mr. Fairchild returned to his estate, and only his mother and Mrs. Harris were at home. The two women were settled cosily in the morning room doing their needlepoint and plying their tongues almost as rapidly as their needles.

"Well, Mother, I believe you thought I should return. Here I am."

"Richard!" Mrs. Fairchild exclaimed, taken by surprise. "I'm certainly glad you did, but I confess I did not expect to see you until this evening at the earliest."

"I got your letter last evening and . . . and I was restless. So I arose early and enjoyed an energetic ride back."

Mrs. Harris rose. "I shall just return to my room for a rest."

"That is considerate of you, Katherine," Mrs. Fairchild said, "but it is unnecessary. If anything, I can use your presence to corroborate anything I have to say about Emma and Melissa."

Mr. Fairchild's lips straightened into a thin line. "Mother, I believe I made a mistake about my proposed marriage. I am going to ask Miss Chadwell to release me from my promise."

"You'll do no such thing! I declare, men!"

"Mother—"

"No! You just listen to me! I have never seen a more natural mother than Emma. And the changes in Melissa! Well, you wouldn't recognise her."

"That is true, Mr. Fairchild," Mrs. Harris quickly supported her friend. "The child has improved all out of reason. Why, she obeys Emma beautifully, and is a happy, normal child since Emma took her in hand."

"I find that hard to believe," Mr. Fairchild replied.

"Only because you have been absent for far too long!"

"I had business to attend to."

"You have slighted Emma."

"Mother, my relationship with Miss Chadwell is between the two of us. I will not tolerate interference."

His mother's sniff opposed his statement, but he ignored it. However, he thought about what she and Mrs. Harris had said. If it were true, then there would be no need to break off the engagement. After all, that had been his intent all along. He wasn't sure why that thought didn't appease the restlessness he had experienced ever since his proposal.

"All right, Mother. I shall postpone my decision until I see whether or not your observations are accurate."

"I think you will be pleased."

"Where is Miss Chadwell now?"

"She and Melissa went on a picnic with Deborah and Lord Atherton in the south meadow. Peters can tell you exactly where if you want to go meet them."

"I've been in the saddle all morning. I think I'll retire to my chamber for fresh attire and do some book work instead. I'll see everyone later."

Mrs. Fairchild was disappointed. She had hoped he would see Emma and the child together before they became aware of his presence.

Mr. Fairchild wandered upstairs to submit to his valet's ministrations, his mind toying with the information his mother had given him. It appeared his mother felt Miss Chadwell capable of raising his child. Certainly, she would be more at ease without her stepmother's presence. Suddenly, he reversed his earlier decision. He would ride out and meet the party.

Deborah was showing Melissa and Emma how to make a daisy chain while Lord Atherton reclined beside her, watching her graceful movements. Emma guided Melissa's little hands to follow Deborah's instructions. When their work of art was completed, Emma crowned Melissa with the fragrant chain atop her golden curls, and both young women clapped at the pretty picture the child made.

"Now, you must make your curtsey, Melissa, just as a princess would."

"I thought everyone else bowed down to a princess," Melissa said, speculation in her eyes.

"But you are not a princess, sweetheart, only a very special little girl," Emma said with a warm smile.

The child curtseyed before collapsing onto Emma's lap with a giggle. "I enjoy being your little girl, Miss Emma. When may I call you Mama?"

Emma cradled Melissa against her bosom, her cheek resting on the child's smooth skin. "I don't know, my pet. Let's just be friends for now."

"But—"

"Hush, child. You must learn patience."

"And that's not an easy thing to learn, Melissa," Lord Atherton chimed in. "Many adults have yet to learn that particular lesson."

"True, James, but it seems to me you are giving an excellent show of it." Mr. Fairchild spoke from among the trees where he had observed the group.

"Mr. Fairchild!" Emma gasped.

"Richard! When did you get back?" Lord Atherton asked.

"About an hour ago. I apologise for my lengthy stay in town, Miss Chadwell, but I had some duties to attend to."

"Of course, Mr. Fairchild. Melissa," Emma prodded the child, who was now hiding her face against her. "Why do you not show your father the flower crown you made with Miss Harris's assistance."

The child, after a week of loving care, minded Emma instinctively, raising her head and standing on her sturdy little legs in front of the tall man. With a nod from Emma, Melissa made a bobbing curtsey and said in a wavery voice, "See, Papa?"

"Very nice, Melissa, and a very nice curtsey, too. I see you learned a great deal while I was away."

"Miss Emma taught me everything!" Melissa quickly told her father while she beamed at the young woman.

"That was very kind of her."

"And . . . and she's going to be my—"

"Melissa!" Emma intervened, uncertain how Mr. Fairchild would react to his daughter's knowledge of his plans, or at least the plans he had at one time. Emma was not at all sure he still intended to carry them out.

Melissa turned to stare at her, tears welling up in her big blue eyes. Emma's heart was wrung, but she reached out a hand to the child and said gently, "Friend, Melissa. I'm going to be your friend."

The child nodded, swallowing her disappointment while the man watched in surprise. Only a week ago, any attempt to thwart the child had resulted in unending tantrums. His mother was right. Miss Chadwell had worked miracles.

"I give you my compliments, Miss Chadwell. You have indeed made a miraculous change in the week I have been gone."

"Nay, sir, not miraculous. I have only loved and been loved in return. Is that not true, Melissa?"

"Yes! I love Miss Emma. And I don't ever want her to leave!" the child added with just a hint of her earlier wilfulness.

"Did you have a successful sojourn in London?" Emma asked in an attempt to change the subject before Melissa lost control.

"Why, yes, I did. I also chanced to see your future sister-in-law from a distance."

"How nice," Emma said.

"Are you not curious about the newest member of your family?"

"Yes, of course."

"Me, too," Deborah added, before blushing at her boldness. "It is just that I have never met Miss Stokie, and we attended many of the Season's events."

"I feel quite sure Miss Stokie was not invited to any of the *ton*'s parties," Mr. Fairchild continued. "Her father is a sausage maker, good yeoman stock but not the kind invited to Almack's."

Emma said nothing, already having known the young woman was not quality.

"She must be worth her weight in gold," Lord Atherton commented without thinking. Then, flushed, he said, "I beg your pardon, Emma. I did not mean . . ."

"It is all right, James. My family's financial needs are well-known."

Mr. Fairchild raised his eyebrows at the familiarity of the party but said nothing.

"Is she pretty?" Deborah asked.

"I fear I cannot respond to that question without appearing ungentlemanly, Miss Harris. Suffice it to say that there is enough of her to make four of you."

Though Deborah's eyes widened and her lips quivered, she did not laugh out loud. Lord Atherton did not have such control, but he quickly turned it into a cough.

"Speaking of beauty, however, I must compliment you on your appearance, Miss Chadwell."

Emma blushed but said a quiet thank-you. Melissa looked at her father curiously, having hardly ever seen him in such a congenial mood. Emboldened by such behaviour, she leaned forward from Emma's lap and asked, "Why do you not call her Emma, like Lord Atherton?"

Emma held her breath, afraid the man would not show patience at the child's interruption, but Mr. Fairchild was no monster. He smiled kindly at his daughter. "It is not polite to address a lady by her first name until she has given permission to do so, Melissa."

"Oh. Miss Emma, may my papa call you by your first name?"

"Yes, of course," Emma said hurriedly, willing the conversation on to some impersonal topic.

"Thank you, Emma. I am pleased to be granted such a privilege."

Lord Atherton, observing their conversation, said, "You should not have gone away as you did, and you would have received that privilege much earlier. We have all decided on first names. We have had a most enjoyable week. The weather has been favourable, and we have spent a lot of time outdoors."

"And I have a pony!" Melissa squealed, remembering the precious animal Peters had introduced to her only that morning.

"I did not know. Is Peters instructing you in the care of your pony?"

"Yes," Melissa said solemnly.

"Then I am glad you have a pony. You must show him to me."

"Now? May I show him to Papa now, Miss Emma?" the little girl demanded.

"Perhaps your father would have time to stop by the stables when we arrive back at the house. And I believe it is time we return, do you not think, Deborah?"

"I am sure you are right, Emma. Only, it is so pleasant here."

"You don't want to go back because you know I will defeat you in spindlepegs this evening," Lord Atherton teased.

"Well, you may defeat me," Deborah challenged, "but you know you don't stand a chance against Emma."

"What is this? You are playing such childish games, James?" Emma flushed, but she was surprised by Mr. Fairchild's next words. "We will see if Emma will remain champion after my challenge."

"Splendid!" James enthused. "And with Richard to even the numbers, we might try our hand at Charades again."

"Let's go now so I can show Papa my pony," Melissa begged, tired of the adult banter.

"All right, love. James, if you will signal Andrew to come carry the baskets, Deborah and I will repack the remains."

Emma had only seen Mr. Fairchild as a member of the *ton*, adhering to its rules. At least, she reminded herself, adhering to most of them. He had overstepped the bounds of propriety several times in his remarks to her. But then, so had she, she admitted to herself. But the sight of Mr. Fairchild roaring with laughter over one of Deborah's more innovative attempts at Charades gave Emma a different view of him.

His behaviour with his child had also made a favourable impression on Emma. He had escorted the little girl into the stables willingly and praised the pony she showed him. That the praise was also directed towards Peters was not obvious to Melissa, and Emma was pleased.

Mr. Fairchild watched Emma as she took her turn in their childish game. For the first time in front of him, she was totally at ease, involved in using her skills to succeed. He was amazed at the difference the warmth of her smile made in her appearance, coupled with the suitable clothing and simple hairstyle. True, she would not be accorded a diamond of the first water by the *ton*, but she was an attractive woman.

"Mr. Fairchild? Mr. Fairchild, have you no guess?" Emma asked him, wondering at his silence.

"What? Oh, yes, of course . . ." He looked at his friend for guidance but received only a knowing grin in return. "You could at least assist me, James, and not leave me to demonstrate my ignorance."

"Not me, my friend. We are on opposite teams."

"Ah. Well, Mother, will you assist me?"

"I could, I suppose, but I think not. You should learn not to let your mind wander."

"Ah! The cruelty of motherhood."

Mrs. Fairchild smiled, but did not hesitate to turn the subject. "At least Melissa will never have reason to cry the cruelty of fate with Emma as her mother."

Emma blushed, but Mr. Fairchild did not respond to his mother's sally. Instead, he made a random guess at the puzzle and returned the conversation to their present occupation.

When Emma went to bed that evening, for the first time she considered with optimism Mr. Fairchild's plan. Already she loved Fairchild House, and even more Melissa and her grandmother. But she had been troubled by a future involving the man whose name was attached to the other two. Now, seeing a new side of him, she could even contemplate accepting his name with equanimity.

Mr. Fairchild was joined by his friend in the library after the women had retired. He handed Lord Atherton a glass of brandy and sat down opposite him with a grimace. "So, how has your week gone?"

"Excellent, Richard. I have never spent a more enjoyable time. The weather has been perfect and my companions beyond compare."

"By companions, I think you must mean Miss Harris."

Lord Atherton ignored the other's teasing smile. "Yes, certainly I mean Miss Harris. She is wonderful, of course. Beautiful, intelligent, warm and gentle." Before Mr. Fairchild could speak, Lord Atherton added, "But I also include the other three ladies and Melissa."

"You have always been a favourite with my mother," Mr. Fairchild said casually.

"Thank you. I also hope I am a favourite with Mrs. Harris, since I intend to make her my mother-in-law."

"What? You are that smitten with the young lady?"

"You seem surprised, and I thought that was your intention when you invited her," Lord Atherton said with some asperity.

Mr. Fairchild frowned. "Perhaps it was . . . but I never thought . . . that is, I felt we needed some company in addition to Mrs. Chadwell. I could not contemplate an entire week in that woman's company without some kind of antidote."

"That is understandable."

"Seriously, James, I was not attempting to trap you into marriage. Surely you cannot believe—"

"Rest easy, Richard. I have been subjected to the presence of more than one young lady, several of them more beautiful than Deborah, though I beg you will not mention that to her," he finished with a warm smile. "If I am caught, it is because I want to be caught. I am too wily about the ways of women for it to be otherwise."

"And you are sure?"

Lord Atherton smiled. "Quite. But please say nothing to the others. I have not yet spoken to Mrs. Harris or . . . or even hinted to Deborah that . . ."

"You have been most circumspect."

"This is important. I want nothing to go wrong."

"And does the young woman return your regard?"

"I hope so. I discussed it with Emma and—"

"With Emma? Why would you take her into your confidence?"

Frowning, Lord Atherton said, "Because she is trustworthy and intelligent . . . and a very nice person," he finished fiercely.

Raising his eyebrows, Mr. Fairchild said, "I meant no criticism, James. I simply thought you had not known her long to make such a judgement."

"I have certainly known her longer and better than you, my friend, and *I* have no intention of marrying her."

Mr. Fairchild rose from his chair to stand by the fireplace and stare down at his friend. "If that was intended as a criticism of me, James, I do not see what I have done to deserve it."

Troubled, Lord Atherton stared down at his drink. "It is just that . . . I don't know, Richard. Your scheme seemed all right when you first told me, but Emma . . . it is different now that I know her."

"What has changed? I am behaving no differently than most members of the *ton*. Marriage is an agreement that benefits both parties. It will keep Miss Chadwell from being an old maid, dependent upon her bankrupt family, and provide her with every comfort. I will receive a mother for my child, and a companion for my mother. It seems a fair agreement."

"Yes, I suppose it is, as long as both parties understand the rules and . . . and it is all you are prepared to settle for."

"Are you saying Miss Chadwell has indicated she is not happy with our agreement?"

"No! No, I'm not saying that. I believe Emma would marry the devil himself to be Melissa's mother. But there is so much more. Do you not look for any affection from your wife? Do you still have the intention of abandoning her and returning to your old life as soon as the marriage takes place?"

"Of course I do. Why would it be otherwise?" Mr. Fairchild stared at his friend, wondering at his thinking, before an explanation occurred to him. "Ah, I see."

"What do you see?"

"You have been caught by a pair of pretty blue eyes and you want me to fall into the same trap. Misery loves company, and all that."

"If this be misery, may I never be free from it."

Mr. Fairchild smiled grimly. "Once I also expressed words similar to that."

"But, Richard, it does not have to be that way! If you both—"

"Tell me in five years, friend. Then I might pay heed to your words."

Lord Atherton took a long drink while he gathered his resources to counter Mr. Fairchild's words, but his friend continued before he could respond. "I came back with the intention of asking Miss Chadwell to release me, but since my return, I've seen that my judgement was sound. She will be perfect for my plans. She has the option of refusing me, you know. I am not going to marry her against her will. But neither am I going to look for that elusive creature, love, in my marriage. That I will find elsewhere."

"Do you not mean lust?"

"Term it what you will, James. It is all the same. And when I discover that it is not permanent, as you will also do, my arrangements are ended in a dignified manner, with satisfaction on both sides, and I go on to another . . . arrangement."

"You take another mistress, you mean. That is not love, Richard. Love is something more."

"As I said before, James, you may convince me of that after you have spent five years with your Miss Harris. If you can then face me and say that you still love her and she still loves you, and you would marry her again, given the opportunity, then . . . perhaps . . . I will believe you."

"But it will then be too late for you and Emma to . . . it will be too late, Richard. Can you not see that?"

"Ah, you are assuming you will be able to make that statement, friend. But you see, I am not." He held up his hand to prevent his friend's retort. "I will even hold my proposal to be the more honest because my expectations are modest. While you, in your bemusement, expect heaven and earth from your Deborah."

"And will receive it," Lord Atherton affirmed staunchly.

"I wish it for you with all my heart, James," Mr. Fairchild assured his friend as he clapped him on his shoulder, "but I must confess I am fearful of the outcome."

= 9 =

EMMA'S BELIEF THAT their marriage might be a happy one seemed to be shared by Mr. Fairchild. As the days progressed, she discovered a congeniality in him that made their companionship enjoyable. She discussed the estate with him, and they both spent time with Melissa.

She was not too involved in her own life to miss the growing feeling between Lord Atherton and Deborah Harris, however. If separated, each watched the door for the other's appearance. If together, they saw only each other.

Emma could not deny the ache in her heart when she saw their love. But she tried to be grateful for what she was offered. Compared to many, she was truly blessed.

Mr. Fairchild seemed unaware of his friend's state of mind, as far as Emma could tell. His attention was turned to more practical matters.

"How is it that you know so much about farming, Emma?" he asked one day after they had joined in a discussion with his manager about the crops being planted.

"I have managed my brother's small estate for a number of years, Mr. . . . er, Richard."

"Did not your brother have some say in its management?"

"No, he had no interest in it."

"Still, he must have conferred with you about the general scheme of things, the crops, the animals."

"No." Emma said nothing more, her lips pressed firmly together.

"But . . . you are a woman."

For the first time since her arrival at Fairchild House, Emma felt less than welcome and unhappy about her situation. "Yes, I am a woman," she confirmed, tight-lipped.

Confused by both her attitude and her words, Mr. Fairchild tried another tack. "Do you have an excellent manager at your brother's estates?"

"We have a manager."

"Yes, but . . . how long has he been there?"

"Old Ben is past seventy."

"Well, his experience must have been very helpful to you." The condescending tones lent aggressiveness to Emma, a trait she had rarely displayed to her intended. "Not nearly as helpful as Mr. Coke's books on farming. His methods are far superior to those used in Old Ben's day. He did have some expertise on the stud farm, but there have been several theories advanced in the past few years that he refused to accept. I implemented them anyway, with very good results."

"You've read Mr. Coke's writings . . . and you managed the stud farm as well? That is no job for a woman!"

Emma's raised her chin in stubborn pride. "I do not see why. I certainly proved a woman could do as well as a man."

"I see." Mr. Fairchild studied the stubborn tilt of her chin. "So you enjoy life in the country?"

"Yes, of course. I much prefer it to life in the city."

"So . . . after our marriage you will not mind if . . . if I sometimes return to town and leave you in charge here with Melissa?"

Had Mr. Fairchild told her his plans more clearly at the time he proposed, Emma would have been greatly relieved. She still preferred the country to the city, but the few days spent while Mr. Fairchild was in residence had shown her she was not as indifferent to him as a man as she had thought. However, she knew the response he wanted and gave it quietly. "I will be delighted to have you place such trust in my abilities, Richard."

"Ah, that is most gracious of you, Emma."

They strolled on in silence, neither having anything to add to their conversation.

After a few minutes, Mr. Fairchild commented, "Melissa is doing very well with her riding lessons. I should have thought of that before, but . . ."

"She needed a more active life."

Mr. Fairchild accepted the unspoken criticism of his handling of his daughter with equanimity. He deserved it, he admitted to himself. "You have made quite a difference in Melissa's behaviour, and I am grateful."

"Yes," Emma said consideringly, some devilish spur causing her to add, "It would've been a shame had I not been able to fill the purpose of our engagement."

Mr. Fairchild considered denying her statement, but her large brown eyes demanded honesty. "You are right, Emma. I did propose marriage to you because of Melissa. But I have not been dishonest with you. I never professed undying love. I offer you a comfortable home and work that you seem to enjoy."

Her eyes falling to the ground, Emma conceded, "I am not complaining, Mr. Fairchild . . . Richard. But I would prefer that we be honest with each other."

"I, too, would prefer honesty between us, Emma. In my first marriage, deceit was prevalent. I would not consider marriage again if I did not believe it would be different this time."

"And that is why you have chosen me, so lacking in looks when compared to the first Mrs. Fairchild."

"I admit you were lacking in looks when I first saw you, but since your arrival here, I have nothing to complain about."

Though pleased with his response, Emma said, "We agreed to be honest, Mr. Fairchild, and I am aware of my shortcomings."

Mr. Fairchild studied the flushed cheek turned away from him, framed by the smooth knot of light-brown hair. "Are you, Emma? And I thought you were to call me Richard?"

"I—I forgot."

"Well, you mustn't do so in front of Mother. She will decide I have been unkind to you and lecture me for hours.

Not only have you won over Melissa, but you also have my mother's full support."

"She is a wonderful lady, Mr. F—Richard. I am so pleased to know that she approves. Have you discussed . . . that is, I believe she understands why—"

"Yes. She understands."

"Good."

"Yes. Honesty all around is the best thing."

When they returned to the house, Mr. Fairchild quite satisfied with their frank discussion, they discovered Lord Atherton had taken advantage of their absence to approach Mrs. Harris about her daughter's hand. Having no objection, of course, to surrendering her daughter to one of the *ton*'s most eligible bachelors, she promptly summoned Deborah and Lord Atherton proposed to his beloved.

The other couple's arrival coincided with their announcement to Mrs. Fairchild, and champagne was ordered to celebrate the happy occasion.

The contrast between the glorious happiness that flowed from Deborah and Lord Atherton and her matter-of-fact agreement caused Emma some pangs, but she successfully hid them and congratulated the younger girl. She was truly happy for the pair of them, sure that they were well-matched.

Mr. Fairchild regarded their ecstasy with a jaundiced eye, his vision blinded by his own experience. He even felt satisfaction that his engagement had been rationally discussed by him and Miss Chadwell, with none of the attendant romantic expectations. It gave him an even greater appreciation of his fiancée.

The house party continued for only two more days, fortunately. Because, while the newly engaged couple grew happier and more in love each moment spent together, Emma and Mr. Fairchild grew stiff and uneasy in their agreement. Emma looked upon the joy of the others as forbidden fruit, knowing it was not for her, but drawn to it more and more. She tried to envision how she would feel if Mr. Fairchild's eyes gazed lovingly on her the moment she entered a room, or if he never left her side, whispering sweet words in her ears.

Mr. Fairchild, on the other hand, grew more impatient with their rapture, seeing it as the devil's trap. He felt uneasy that his friend was venturing down a path he had previously travelled to disaster, but he was unable to stop him.

Mrs. Fairchild observed the changing moods of her son and his guests and wondered what the outcome would be. She did not want to lose Emma as her daughter-in-law, but she also ached for the girl's loss in accepting her son's offer.

Would she never know love, know the touch of a man who truly loved her? But she knew her son needed the stability Emma presented him and that her grandchild's happiness depended on it.

The summons for Emma to return to London to attend her brother's wedding came earlier than expected. It arrived in the form of a letter from her mother, raving about the charm of her daughter-in-law-to-be and the generosity of her son. As if it were an afterthought, she commanded Emma's appearance in London the next day.

Emma read the letter with foreboding, dreading the return to her family after enjoying the relaxed atmosphere of Fairchild House. Apologising for the short notice, she explained her mother's request.

"We are sorry for your visit to end, but there is no problem about returning tomorrow, Emma, if that is necessary."

"Yes," Emma assured Mr. Fairchild breathlessly, "Mama says the wedding is to take place in three weeks' time."

"Very well, I'll order the carriage for in the morning."

"I do wish you did not have to leave, Emma. We have grown so comfortable with you here. And Melissa will be devastated," Mrs. Fairchild said.

"Thank you, ma'am. I have loved my visit here . . . and . . . I look forward to my return," Emma said shyly, her marriage still not a reality to her.

Mr. Fairchild returned from passing his orders on to Mrs. Quigley. "I believe we need to discuss the date for our own marriage before you return to town, Emma."

"Oh . . . oh, of course."

Mrs. Harris rose. "Come, Deborah, James. Let us go to the billiard room and James can display his expertise in that senseless game." Her smile signified her teasing, and the other two joined in her laughing.

Mrs. Fairchild waited until they had left the room before saying, "If you would like to discuss this in private, I will be glad to leave also. I do not think your mother would object, Emma, since the two of you are engaged."

"Oh, no—"

"I think it would help if you remained, Mother. I see no sense in delaying our wedding more than two weeks beyond Mr. Chadwell's, and your help in planning would be welcome."

"In five weeks? But that is impossible, Richard! There are Emma's brideclothes, the invitations . . ."

Emma's cheeks flushed crimson as she remembered her brother's feelings about purchasing a trousseau for his sister. Neither had Mr. Fairchild forgotten.

"Brideclothes will not be necessary, Mother," he said with emphasis, hopeful his mother would not question his words. "After all, there is no need for an extensive wardrobe before her marriage. Emma will be able to buy anything she pleases after the wedding."

The wording of his statement halted the protest Mrs. Fairchild had intended to voice. She could not believe the girl's family would treat her so shabbily, but that appeared to be the message her son was trying to convey.

"And as for invitations, I do not believe Emma has a large acquaintance among the *ton*, and I have few friends I want to attend. Certainly Mrs. and Miss Harris and James, and one or two others whom I can personally invite."

Mrs. Fairchild studied Emma's downcast eyes before casually agreeing with her son. She added, "I wonder, Emma, if you would care to be married from Fairchild House? After all, your mother will be recovering from the excitement of your brother's marriage, and I would love the opportunity to fuss over the bride."

Emma smiled gratefully at the woman. "I would love to be married from here if you do not mind, Mrs. Fairchild.

My mother will truly be tired out from the other wedding."

"It would give me great pleasure, child. I shall write your mother a note for you to . . . No! If you do not mind, Richard, I believe I shall accompany you to town. I shall need a new dress to wear to my son's wedding."

"We should be delighted by your presence in town, Mother. But will Melissa be all right here by herself?"

"Of course. Mrs. Quigley will care for her. I shall miss her, but as long as she knows both Emma and I will return, she will be a good girl," Mrs. Fairchild assured her son with a laugh.

"I believe I will absent myself when you tell her that the two of you will be leaving," Mr. Fairchild said dryly.

"I shall miss her very much," Emma assured the other two. "She has been . . . she has given me so much joy."

"I am glad to hear you say that, child. I am looking forward to having more grandchildren soon."

Emma's eyes widened in surprise before she cast a surreptitious look at her fiancé. Mr. Fairchild changed the subject. "Had you not better begin preparations if we are to leave in the morning, Mother?"

"Oh, my, yes! I must discuss my plans with Mrs. Quigley. And I must inform Katherine and Deborah of my decision to accompany all of you. Shall you and James ride, or shall I order a third carriage?"

"I'm sure we'll ride, Mother. We shall be cooped up enough upon our arrival in the city."

Emma descended from Mr. Fairchild's carriage with a sigh. The warmth of Mrs. Fairchild, the love and friendship Mrs. Harris and Deborah shared, the love that had exuded from Deborah and Lord Atherton had made the past few days a joy. Now she must return to the reality of her stepmother and her brother and failing finances.

Mr. Fairchild stood staring down at her hesitation, and Emma became aware of his questioning regard. "Thank you for your escort. I . . . perhaps I will see you—"

"Of course. I will call on you on the morrow, Emma, to see how you are settling in."

The door opened in response to his knock, and he surprised her by placing a kiss on her hand in front of the butler. "Until tomorrow, Miss Chadwell."

Emma cradled her hand against her as she watched Mr. Fairchild turn away and signal the carriage carrying his mother and the Harrises to continue. He swung himself onto his mount and set off down the busy London street, looking back only once to lift a hand in good-bye.

Turning to stare up at the town house, Emma gave another sigh before she followed the footmen who came to remove her trunks from the street.

"Is my stepmother home, Walters?"

"No, Miss Chadwell. Mrs. Chadwell is paying some calls. Mr. Chadwell requested your presence when you arrived, however. He is waiting in the parlour."

Her brother was seated on the sofa, a drink in his hands, when Emma opened the door. However, his eager greeting when he discovered she had returned would have satisfied the most demanding of sisters. It made Emma extremely suspicious. "I am glad you are happy over my return, Charlie. It is more than I expected."

Charlie had the grace to blush. "I may not have always shown my affection for you, Emma, but I do care for you, you know. I just wanted to assure myself of your happiness."

"That's not what you said when I begged you not to bring me to London."

"Now, Emma, that's water under the bridge. I had no choice, especially with Mama harping at me all day long. Anyway, it's turned out well. You can't tell me you ain't happy with Mr. Fairchild."

Emma did not want to answer her brother on that subject. She was becoming more confused each day about her feelings for her fiancé. "I believe I should congratulate you on your engagement, Charlie." She hesitated, but could not stop herself from asking, "Are you sure you are doing the right thing?"

"Don't be a twit, Emma. Of course I am. We can't live on air, you know."

"But Charlie, we were doing all right as long as I remained in the country, running the estate. Why did you . . ."

"Now, Emma, don't start on that again. Besides, what's done is done. You're engaged to Mr. Fairchild and I'm engaged to Miss Stokie. There's no changing that."

"But will you be happy, Charlie?"

Emma's heart ached for him, in spite of her dissatisfaction with his behaviour.

He shrugged his shoulders. "Miss Stokie's not too bad, Emma. And I can't live without money to spend. I don't want to be buried in the country, like you."

"Very well, Charlie. I'm going to lie down now," Emma said, feeling overwhelmed by her return.

"Wait! I wanted to see you to discover if you have set the date for the wedding."

"Yes, we have. It will be two weeks after yours."

"Two weeks after? Why are you waiting so long?"

"So long?" Emma repeated, confused. "Mrs. Fairchild was surprised that we would need only five weeks to prepare."

"But Emma—" Charlie stopped, frustration writ upon his face. He jumped from the sofa to pace the floor.

"What is it, Charlie?"

"Nothing! It is just . . . Emma, I need the marriage settlements before my wedding."

"What?"

Charlie's cheeks were flushed, and he refused to look his sister in the eye. "I need the money now. My future father-in-law expects me to entertain his daughter and introduce her to the *ton*. And . . . and I need to buy her gifts. I can't expect him to provide money for those things, now, can I?"

"I suppose not, but surely he is aware of your financial situation."

"He knows I'm not plump in the pocket, but he doesn't know my pocket is completely to let."

"But, Charlie . . ."

"So, I want you to tell Mr. Fairchild that you want to be married at once. He can get a special licence and take care of everything right and tight."

"I will not!"

"Emma—"

"Do not think you can threaten me, Charlie. What will you do, send me back to the country?"

"Please, Emma, think of me. You want me to be happy, don't you?" Charlie wheedled when he realised threats would not work.

"Yes, I want you to be happy, Charlie, but I will not demand that Mr. Fairchild marry me at once in order to pay for your foolishness."

"But what will I do?"

Emma refused to be moved by his plaintive question. "I think the best thing would be to sell your high-perch phaeton and some of the excuses you have for horses in your stables. And if that does not generate enough coin, you should talk to our man of business about selling out what little we have in the funds. After all, according to you, you will have no money worries after your marriage."

"Why should I make such sacrifices when you only have to marry a few weeks early to save me from that?"

"Because I will not do it," Emma insisted.

"We'll see about that! I'll explain to Mama that you will not assist me in this, and she will make you!"

"She cannot."

"No, but she can ask Mr. Fairchild herself. That's the ticket. I'll get Mama to speak to him."

Humiliation flooded Emma at such a thought. But she refused to beg. "You may do whatever you please, Charlie, but I will have nothing to do with such a plan." With a swish of her skirts, Emma swept from the room, slamming the door behind her. She ran up the stairs to reach the sanctuary of her room. But even there, she could not shut out her brother's words. Surely her stepmother would not humiliate her so. But she knew better. Whenever her brother had demanded something of hers in the past, her stepmother had forced her to comply. This time would be no different.

Several hours later, Emma was summoned to the parlour by her stepmother. When she entered, she realised she should fortify herself for a battle. Mrs. Chadwell was seated on the sofa with Emma's stepbrother, their hands clasped.

"Emma, how could you refuse to help your brother after all he has done for you?"

"What has he done for me, Mama?"

"Why, child, he has housed and clothed you, at his own expense. He has given you a Season that enabled you to snare a very wealthy husband. He has done everything a brother should. And now, in his hour of need, you have refused him. I find it hard to believe you could be so selfish."

Emma sighed. "Mama, I have more than earned my keep with my work on the estate. And I was brought to London for a Season against my will. Mr. Fairchild was accepted without any consideration of my desires. Now you are asking me to humiliate myself by asking my fiancé to marry me in unreasonable haste because my brother is a spend-thrift."

"Emma! How can you say such things about your brother. Charlie has managed very well on the little he has. It is just not fair that other young men have more than he to spend."

"Mama, I cannot ask Mr. Fairchild to marry me out of hand. It would be . . . be unseemly. We have set the wedding day for two weeks after Charlie's wedding."

"Well, it will have to be changed."

"Not by me," Emma insisted determinedly.

"You would defy me, Emma?" her stepmother demanded in a terrible voice.

"Yes, Mama, I would."

"Then go to your room and do not emerge from it until you are prepared to be reasonable." Her chin raised, Emma walked from the room and ascended the stairs. Better her room than in the company of such self-centered relatives, she decided. But she thought back longingly to the past few days when she had enjoyed pleasant company and delicious freedom. She wished she could ask Mr. Fairchild to hasten the wedding so she could return to Fairchild House.

= 10 =

RICHARD FAIRCHILD CALLED on his fiancée the very next day only because he promised her he would, he assured himself. It had nothing to do with the forlorn look she had cast upon him as he last departed. In spite of his assurances to himself, he was almost too early for a polite social call.

Mrs. Chadwell greeted him pleasantly, but his future brother-in-law frowned at him. "I hoped to see Miss Chadwell this morning to satisfy myself that she did not have any ill effects from our return journey," he said, ignoring the other man's bad mood.

"How kind of you, Mr. Fairchild. Unfortunately, Emma has come down with another cold, and it may be several days before she is up and about again."

"Excuse me, Mr. Fairchild, but I have an appointment. Mama, you will not forget our earlier discussion, will you?" the young man asked pointedly.

"No, of course not, my dear." After her son had left the room, Mrs. Chadwell cleared her throat and said, "I understand that you have chosen the second week after Charlie's marriage for your wedding, Mr. Fairchild."

"That is correct. I hope it is acceptable to you, Mrs. Chadwell. I realise it is rather soon after Mr. Chadwell's nuptials, and we can delay it if—"

"No!" Mrs. Chadwell broke in. "No, that is no problem, Mr. Fairchild. In fact, I would have preferred it take place before Charlie's wedding so it would not distract me from that wonderful day."

Mr. Fairchild wondered at the woman's piercing look and

even more at her careless disregard of her stepdaughter's approaching marriage. Stiffly, he replied, "I think such haste would invite undue talk, Mrs. Chadwell. My mother has requested that the wedding take place at Fairchild House, and I'm sure she will undertake to relieve you of all the tiresome details."

"That—that is most gracious of her, I'm sure. If you can wait that long for your bride, I'm sure it is of no moment to me," she concluded with another piercing stare.

"If you have any doubts about my affections for Emma, perhaps you would prefer that we postpone our marriage indefinitely. I know you would not want to bestow your daughter's hand where it might not be appreciated." The smile on his face covered the grim certainty that for some reason he was being pushed to move up the marriage date.

"No! No, not at all. I have no doubts. The second week after Charlie's wedding will be wonderful," Mrs. Chadwell babbled, afraid she might have lost her daughter's wealthy suitor.

"Then we shall consider it settled," he said, rising. "I shall call on Miss Chadwell in another few days. Please give her my best wishes for her immediate recovery."

"Yes, of course. So kind of you to call."

Mr. Fairchild left the Chadwell establishment disappointed. Though he hated to admit it, memories of their halcyon days at Fairchild House made him eager to see her again.

He set thoughts of Emma aside and went to his club for a few hands of cards before a visit to Tattersall's. He had promised Peters to take a look at a brood mare with good lines that was supposed to be put up for sale.

Throughout the day, however, thoughts of Emma remained with him. He realised again how fortunate he was to have found the perfect mother for his child. Now that his mother had the dressing of her, remaking some of her old gowns, Emma was quite attractive also. Her smile lit up her face, and her brown eyes shone with wit and warmth.

Examining the mare, Mr. Fairchild smiled as he imagined

Emma's comments. Her knowledge of farming and animals still amazed him. She would approve of his choice, he knew, and he was eager to discuss it with her. In fact, once they had married, he felt sure he would pay many visits to the estate, conferring with his wife about the management of it and about Melissa.

That evening, after joining friends at his club, Mr. Fairchild strolled down the dark London streets, his mind again turned to Emma. His mother's remark about more grandchildren had teased him frequently. Perhaps it would be better to have more children. It would be good for Melissa.

Emma looked up as the door to her bedchamber opened. Only Nancy had entered her room for several days, and the only meals served had consisted of stale bread and water.

"Well, miss, have you come to your senses?" Mrs. Chadwell demanded, walking over to stare down at Emma with her hands on her hips. Charlie followed her, glaring at his sister.

Emma only nodded no. She had little energy and no interest in their demands.

Mrs. Chadwell blew out her breath in disgust. Charlie edged closer to his mother.

"If you'd just let me take the whip to her, she'd agree."

Though she flinched, Emma said nothing.

"We mustn't do anything to arouse the Fairchilds' suspicions. His mother is already asking too many questions."

"Mrs. Fairchild has called?" Emma asked, showing animation for the first time.

"Called? She's made a downright nuisance of herself." A shrewd look popped into Mrs. Chadwell's eyes. "The next time she calls, I will tell her you no longer want to marry her son. What do you think of that?"

Though her heart squeezed painfully, Emma remained firm. "I think you are pretending. But if you do so, I will return to the estate and be content." She turned her face away from her tormentors and stared out the window, as she had done much of the time she'd spent in her room.

A month ago, she would have welcomed such punishment. Now she wanted to marry Mr. Fairchild and live at Fairchild House with Melissa and her grandmother. But she could do nothing at the moment.

"I told you it would not work!" Charlie snarled.

"Well, I have no more ideas. I cannot believe you can be so stubborn and cruel, Emma. Your brother needs the money from your settlement."

Emma gave no response, refusing to look at them.

"Charlie, you will just have to sell your phaeton to raise the funds. And you may rest assured this young lady will receive no additions to her wardrobe. She'll have to go to her husband as she is!" Mrs. Chadwell laughed angrily. "Mayhap her future husband will realise she is no beauty and will leave her at the altar."

That thought panicked Charlie. "No, Ma, we don't want that! But you will never be welcome in my home again, sister dear, now that you have shown your selfishness. Don't come pleading to me if you are in need."

Emma stared up at her family, pale-faced, her eyes glazed over with weakness, and said nothing.

The other two frowned at each other. "You'd better get some food in her, Ma, or she'll never be ready to drive out with Mrs. Fairchild."

"Ring for Nancy and tell her to bring up a tray. Make it a breakfast tray. I'll make sure she eats before Nancy dresses her."

Mrs. Chadwell held her silence until Emma had eaten several scones and some scrambled eggs. When Emma pushed the tray away from her, she pushed it back. "No, you must eat everything, Emma. I don't want Mrs. Fairchild thinking you in poor health."

"Mama, I cannot," Emma said faintly.

"Don't argue with me. I am too angry with you as it is. It is not good for my health." She sniffed in self-pity and waved at the tray. "You must leave nothing. And if you even hint to Mrs. Fairchild that we have not treated you well, I will cast you out into the streets!"

As if she would tell anyone how her family had treated her, Emma thought shamefully. She could only hope the days would pass swiftly until her wedding day. Where once she had dreaded it, now she prayed for its speedy arrival.

Though she tarried over her food as long as possible, unable to eat so much after her fast, her stepmother insisted she be waiting in the parlour when Mrs. Fairchild returned.

When Mrs. Fairchild arrived, she smiled warmly at the young lady, happy to see her again. But as the slender figure standing by the window turned to face her guest, she frowned.

"Emma, my dear, are you feeling quite the thing? I did not really believe you have been so ill. I am sorry."

"No, dear Mrs. Fairchild. I am not really ill, just a little pulled. I am a terrible invalid, I'm afraid," she said shakily. "Thank you for calling."

Mrs. Fairchild looked at the young woman closely, thinking she appeared to have lost weight since she arrived in London only two days previously, and her skin was pale. The older woman took her hand and led her over to the couch.

"My child, if there is anything I can do, I will be glad to help you."

"There is nothing, Mrs. Fairchild."

The older woman offered a ride in the park to put some colour in Emma's cheeks. Grateful for the chance to escape the reproachful atmosphere in her home, Emma readily accepted.

"Then fetch a shawl, child, so you will not take additional chill, and we will be on our way. Richard's coachman does not like to keep the horses standing."

Emma left the room and Mrs. Fairchild thought about their interview. If Emma's cold had been so severe as to do the damage shown in the young woman's face, it appeared to the older woman there would still be evidence of it. She thought of the rosy, happy face Emma had evidenced while playing with Melissa and laughing with the other young people. She did not seem so happy now.

They had almost completed their way around the park when Mrs. Fairchild broached the subject of Emma's wardrobe, offering to purchase her brideclothes for her. She was not surprised when the young lady refused to even consider the idea.

"No, thank you, ma'am. I have enough clothes for . . . for everything."

"Emma, my son's wife must be properly dressed. After all, he will expect it."

"Mrs. Fairchild, Mr. Fairchild explained that I would be remaining in the country. I have sufficient wardrobe for that for quite some time."

"Emma, has Richard done something to put you off? You do not seem as happy as you were at Fairchild House."

Her cheeks burning, Emma said, "Of course not, ma'am. It is only that I miss Melissa and everyone. Mr. Fairchild has been wonderful to me. But it is true that I will not be in London much after our marriage. You know he is marrying me to provide a mother for Melissa."

"I know my son is a fool," the woman muttered.

"I beg your pardon?"

"Nothing, child. I am just distressed to see you unhappy. But you must think about those gowns. It would give me great pleasure."

Emma was distressed to deny this kind lady any pleasure, but she was sure her family would protest if she gained anything from her betrothal that did not benefit them. And she was weary of the constant turmoil.

Richard Fairchild looked up as the door to the library opened and then got to his feet as his mother entered.

"Richard! You must do something about Emma."

"What are you talking about, Mother?" Mr. Fairchild asked calmly as he laid down his pen and closed the accounts book he had been studying.

"I just came from taking Emma for a drive. I want to purchase her some new gowns, and she refuses to allow me to do so. And besides, she is not happy."

Mr. Fairchild frowned. "What do you mean?"

"Emma is pale from her cold," her mother said. "But she does not smile as she did at Fairchild House."

"Did you ask her if anything was wrong?"

"Of course I did. But she only said she missed Melissa."

Walking over to his mother, Richard Fairchild took her hands to comfort her. "You have been telling me Melissa was loveable. Now that you have found someone to love her, you are complaining about it." She did not smile at his teasing. With a sigh, he said, "I will go visit Emma today. I did not realise she had recovered from her cold."

"And you will convince her to let me take her shopping? It would mean so much to me, dear," she assured her son.

"I will do my best. But you know, I believe Emma is a strong woman. I cannot guarantee success."

"I know. And see if you can convince her to smile more. She is such a dear child."

"All right, Mother. I'm glad you are pleased with my choice. I will let you know if I am successful."

His mother smiled in approval, and he escorted her to the stairs. He stood watching as she ascended. She had grown old while he had not been watching, he thought. He motioned to his butler. "Send a bottle of sherry up to Mrs. Fairchild along with some biscuits."

"Yes, Mr. Fairchild. Shall I bring refreshments to you in the library also?"

"What? Oh, no. Call my curricle around. I am going out."

When he was shown into the Chadwells' parlour, it was Mrs. Chadwell rather than Emma who occupied it.

"La, Mr. Fairchild. It is rather late in the day to be paying social calls. I'm afraid Emma is lying down, and I do hate to disturb her. She is still recovering from her cold, you know."

Mr. Fairchild put on his most charming smile and greeted the woman. "I do apologise, Mrs. Chadwell, but I have not seen Emma since our return to the city. Would it be possible to speak to her for just a few minutes?"

"Well . . . as I was young once myself, I suppose I could have her called down. But you must make it a short stay. She is really pulled by this cold."

Mrs. Chadwell stepped from the room and then immediately returned. "I have sent for her, Mr. Fairchild. I suppose you do have things to discuss since your wedding is following so quickly on the heels of Charlie's. My, I am that excited by Charlie's marriage. She is a lucky girl, let me tell you."

"Yes, I'm sure she is, Mrs. Chadwell. Almost as lucky as I feel to be marrying Emma."

"Oh, well, yes, of course, though Emma doesn't compare to my Aurora, you know. But she's . . . she's a quiet girl. She should give you no trouble."

"No, I'm sure she won't."

The door opened again, and this time Emma appeared. Mr. Fairchild agreed with his mother that she still seemed pale. And there was no smile on her face at his presence. Had she changed her mind? "Good afternoon, Miss Chadwell. I'm sorry to hear you have been burdened with a cold."

"Thank you, Mr. Fairchild," Emma said.

"Emma, dear, where are your manners? The gentleman cannot be seated until you are. Come over here and sit on the sofa so Mr. Fairchild can join you. After all, he was most insistent on seeing you," she added coyly.

Emma moved to do her stepmother's bidding, but there was no discernible emotion in her face. Mr. Fairchild followed, sitting beside her.

"How do you feel, Miss Chadwell?" he asked, hesitant to use her first name in front of her mother.

"Fine, thank you."

"Your mother said when I called after our return that you had caught a cold on the return journey."

"Yes."

Mr. Fairchild flicked a glance at Mrs. Chadwell, wishing he could think of a reason for them to be alone. Mrs. Chadwell misinterpreted his look.

"I do apologise for Emma, Mr. Fairchild. She's never been one for conversation. She prefers the fields at home to a ballroom. Now, my Aurora, she's a beauty, and she knows how to entertain a man. It is certainly a shame she is already married. You would've been so taken with her."

"I have no complaints about Emma's behaviour, Mrs.

Chadwell, but I am concerned about her health. I wonder if I might have a few minutes alone with her. After all, we are engaged."

"Well, I don't rightly think that would be proper. After all, you wouldn't be the first young man who's been a little too eager for his bride," the woman said archly.

Mr. Fairchild simply stared at Mrs. Chadwell, one eyebrow raised in contempt, which caused the woman to say hurriedly, "Emma really should be resting after her excursion with your mother. Why do you not call tomorrow and take her for a ride."

=== 11 ===

EMMA WAS WAITING for Richard the next day when he arrived. Not only was she eager to see him, but also her stepmother was growing uncomfortable around the man. She complained to Emma that he had almost gone beyond acceptable behaviour the day before.

"If we didn't need his money so badly," she'd muttered, "I would not let you marry him. Aurora's husband has exquisite manners."

Though Emma knew her stepmother would not end the engagement, the threats were wearing. She was stronger today, having had several meals now, but she still felt shaky.

The piercing look Mr. Fairchild gave her as he entered didn't help her composure.

"Good morning, Miss Chadwell. I hope you are feeling better this morning."

"Yes, thank you, Mr. Fairchild," she said, smiling.

"Will you accompany me on a ride in the park? I have brought the laudalet today. I thought it might be more comfortable than my curricle."

"Yes, thank you."

"You see, Mr. Fairchild, I told you Emma would be better today. She has even fetched her shawl so as to not keep you waiting." Mrs. Chadwell smiled brightly at the man. Assisting her daughter with the shawl, she warned in a whisper, "Not a word of complaint or you will regret it."

Emma pressed her lips together and drew her shawl closer to her. Did her stepmother think she wanted people to know of their treatment of her? Without a word to either of the others, she walked through the door. Mr. Fairchild bid Mrs. Chadwell farewell and followed on her heels.

No conversation ensued until after they had arrived at Hyde Park. In the meantime, Mr. Fairchild watched Emma relax in the unusually warm sunshine and a smile return to her lips.

"I am delighted you have recovered from your cold. Both my mother and I were concerned about you."

Emma thanked him for his concern but sought for another topic of conversation. She did not want to lie to him, but she could not reveal the source of her illness.

"Are you quite warm?" he asked solicitously.

"Oh, yes. It is such a glorious day, one could not take cold today, Mr. Fairchild," she assured him with a wide smile.

"Richard. And I'm glad we are in agreement." He smiled down at her. "It will relieve my mother greatly to know that you are feeling better. Of course, she is still upset that you will not allow her to buy you any new gowns."

"But Mr. Fair—Richard! I cannot let your mother do that."

"Why not? It is her greatest wish."

"But . . . but we are not yet married."

"Of course not. Once we are married, I will buy all your gowns."

Emma did not know what to say. Her family would protest if she received expensive gifts and yet would not assist them. And her marriage to Mr. Fairchild still seemed a dream. "What—what if we don't marry? I wouldn't be able to pay her back."

Richard turned to stare at her, and Emma was glad he did not have the reins in his hands. "What are you talking about, Emma? Why would we not marry?"

"You . . . one of us might change our mind."

"Not me. Do you have any intention of changing your mind?"

"No! Of course not. It is my fondest wish to become Melissa's mother—and your wife."

Giving a wry laugh, Mr. Fairchild conceded, "Well, at least I believe the part about Melissa."

Alarmed that he might think she did not desire the marriage, Emma tried again. "Truly, Mr. Fairchild! I am looking forward to our marriage."

Mr. Fairchild smiled at her response, pleased in spite of himself. "I am delighted to hear it, Emma. It might be a little more convincing if you remembered to call me Richard, however."

"Richard. I meant Richard."

Mr. Fairchild reached out to pat her hand. "Good. I, too, am looking forward to our marriage. Now, back to my mother. It would please me very much, Emma, if you would allow Mother to indulge herself by purchasing you several things. She never had a daughter, and she would enjoy it. It is her own money she will be spending, you know. I am not secretly financing your trousseau, if that is what is worrying you."

"No, but I do not know how my stepmother will react. And—and I am still not sure it is the correct thing to do. I would not want to cause talk."

"My dear innocent," Mr. Fairchild laughed, "we have been causing talk ever since we met. But there is nothing improper about this, and you must tell your stepmother that it is a present from your future mother-in-law. I do not believe she will care."

Emma could not resist both his persuasion and the thought of new gowns chosen by someone with excellent taste. She sighed and then agreed. "All right. I would be pleased to accept."

"Good girl. And this ride has done you some good. I begin to see pale roses in your cheeks."

Emma smiled but made no comment in return. It was impossible to explain her situation . . . and besides, those roses were due as much to her companion as to the fresh air.

Emma's first shopping trip with Mrs. Fairchild was an enlightening experience. Though her stepmother might buy an elaborate bonnet on a whim, the money for Emma's clothes had always been calculated to the penny.

When Emma first protested her future mother-in-law's

selections, Mrs. Fairchild looked at her in puzzlement. "Do you not care for my choices, my dear? If not, feel free to—"

"Oh, no!" Emma protested. "It's not that. You have exquisite taste. But—but it's too much. Truly, I don't need all these things."

Having already discovered the sacrificial nature of this young woman, Mrs. Fairchild did not misunderstand her protest. However, in spite of her well-marshalled arguments, she would have failed to persuade Emma without the unexpected assistance of Miss Harper.

The young woman strolled into the modiste's waiting room, surrounded by several friends. When she spotted Mrs. Fairchild and her charge, she greeted the older woman and nodded to Emma. Turning away, she whispered to her friends in a voice meant to be overheard, "I cannot understand what he sees in her. She's always foolishly dressed. Look at those outlandish ruffles! And that shade of green makes her look like a sick cow! Too, too droll!" With trills of laughter, the trio strolled out.

Mrs. Fairchild looked at Emma's white face with concern. However, her attempt to console the young lady was unnecessary.

"It is all right, Mrs. Fairchild. Miss Harper is quite right. I am a figure of fun in these ridiculous dresses." She steadied her lower lip with even, white teeth.

Fighting back the urge to hug her, Mrs. Fairchild only said, "All the more reason to dress appropriately now. It will give me great pleasure and reflect well on your new family."

"Very well. I place myself in your hands," Emma said lightly, hiding the turmoil inside.

Needing no more encouragement, Mrs. Fairchild became a whirlwind of activity, eagerly assisted by Mademoiselle Joie, a true Frenchwoman among the many pretenders in the world of fashion. With visions of a large order and the challenge of dressing one not considered a beauty but with a slender form, the Frenchwoman joined with Mrs. Fairchild in completing the transformation of Emma from a country miss to an elegant woman of fashion.

Though most of the garments would be delivered over the next week, Emma still found herself surrounded by packages as Mrs. Fairchild's carriage returned her to her home. Several simple gowns had been ordered for her immediate use, and then there were the slippers, gloves, ribbons and bonnets that Mrs. Fairchild had deemed necessary.

Emma basked in the glow of owning such undreamed of finery as she watched the footman carry her packages into the house. It was only natural to wonder if her betrothed would notice the change in her appearance.

"What is this?" Mrs. Chadwell's shrill voice interrupted her dreams.

"Mr. Fairchild's mother wanted to buy me some—some additions to my wardrobe as a gift, Mama," Emma said quietly.

As predicted by the Fairchilds, Emma's stepmother could scarcely forbid such kindness.

"Hmmph! It seems very coldhearted that you should be sporting such finery when your poor brother is short of funds!" A speculative gleam came into Mrs. Chadwell's eye. "Mayhap some of your new gewgaws will make a fine gift for Charlie to give Miss Stokie."

"It would be difficult for me to explain the disappearance of any of it, since it was all chosen by Mrs. Fairchild," Emma said coolly.

"Coldhearted, just like I said!"

Emma turned to follow her packages up the stairs. Mrs. Chadwell reached out to grab her arm. "I'm coming up with you, young lady. I must inspect these purchases to be sure they are proper for an innocent young girl!"

Holding back an angry retort, Emma continued up the stairs. Half an hour later, when every package had been opened and thrown down in disarray, Mrs. Chadwell protested, "I declare! I have never seen such a collection of poor-spirited gifts. Why, even the parasol has only one ruffle! Does that woman have no taste? It is all so plain. Why, even in her day dresses, Miss Stokie is much more elaborate."

Emma controlled her shudder with an effort. She had yet to meet her brother's intended, but if her stepmother thought her very fashionable, Emma was not looking forward to the meeting.

"You can keep your gifts. Even your brother, since your meanness forced him to sell his carriage, can afford better than this." The irritated woman turned to go, only saying over her shoulder, "I wouldn't wear too many of these things. People will think you have no style at all."

Emma released a deep sigh as the door closed behind her stepmother. She rose and rang for Nancy to help her restore order while she silently gave thanks for the marriage she had protested only a short time ago.

The next few days restored Emma's enjoyment of life. The new gowns made a difference in her appearance and she felt increased confidence when she moved among the *ton*, no longer thinking of herself as an outsider.

During the days, she accompanied Mrs. Fairchild on more shopping expeditions. Not only were they buying clothes for Emma, but there were presents to purchase for Melissa, odds and ends for Fairchild House, and special purchases for friends at home.

Emma had never realised how much fun shopping could be, particularly when one did not have to count every penny and worry about whether the bills could be paid.

It was almost a week after their first shopping expedition that Emma ventured out with Mrs. Fairchild to evening entertainment, not wanting to appear until she could do so in her new finery. In all of that time, Mr. Fairchild had been curiously absent.

"He has a great deal of work, child," Mrs. Fairchild assured Emma one afternoon when she hesitantly enquired about her fiancé. "I am sure he does not mean to neglect you." Neither woman met the other's eyes.

"Of course not," Emma murmured.

When the ball gowns arrived, Emma prepared for her first evening on the town since her return from Fairchild House. The icy blue tissue that was elegantly draped over the matching silk underskirt floated around her as she turned in front of the mirror. Her aquamarine drop was nestled between the swell of her breasts, decorously exposed by the gown's neckline, and her hair was swept up in an intricate knot newly discovered by Nancy.

"Lovey, you are truly a sight this evening," Nancy whispered as she stared in awe at her mistress.

Emma twisted and turned before the mirror, determined to see every inch from the matching ribbon in her hair to the tip of her ice-blue slippers. "I am much improved, am I not, Nancy?"

"Mercy, yes. Mr. Fairchild will be that proud to have you on his arm."

The sparkle in Emma's eyes dimmed slightly, but she raised her chin and smiled firmly. "Yes, I believe he will."

He certainly couldn't be any less proud than when he had sat beside her the evening he proposed. With her shoulders back and a confident smile on her lips that hid her tremors of uncertainty, Emma descended the stairs to await the Fairchilds' arrival.

"You must pay special attention to Emma this evening," Mrs. Fairchild instructed her only son as the carriage stopped in front of the Chadwells'.

"Why?"

Looking with disgust at the man beside her, Mrs. Fairchild said, "Because you have neglected her since our return to London and because all of Society will be watching the both of you."

"Mother, I told you I had a great deal of work to do," Richard Fairchild protested.

"Yes, of course," his mother replied dryly.

Retreat seemed the best response, and Mr. Fairchild opened the carriage door. "Wait here while I fetch Emma." He jumped down from the carriage in relief. At least once his fiancée joined them, his mother would refrain from her lectures. Sometimes he thought she seemed more concerned about Emma than her own child.

He waited in the hall for Emma to join him, his thoughts on business problems, with no anticipation whatsoever for the evening before him. He was only in attendance because his mother had insisted. After all, this was not a normal engagement, and he did not expect to be required to do the pretty every evening.

"I am ready, Richard."

He turned to discover Emma standing across the hall. While not an expert on women's finery, he recognised the elegance of her appearance. She would never be a beauty, but there was an air of confidence about her, sorely missing when he had first met her, that would make her stand out among the debutantes.

"You appear to advantage this evening, Emma," Richard assured her, feeling he had done his duty.

Emma acknowledged the compliment with a smile, but inside, that flutter of hope that had grown when she viewed herself in the mirror died a swift death. Foolish dreams. He wanted a mother for his child, nothing more. She would do well to remember it.

The couple joined Mrs. Fairchild in the carriage.

Emma's new appearance was noted by the *ton* that evening, as well as Mrs. Fairchild's staunch support. Suddenly, Emma was no longer an outsider looking in. She had become one of the elite. That evening set the tone for Emma's second Season, as she considered it to be. Of course, that did not stop those like Miss Harper from making spiteful remarks.

It was one such remark, overheard by Mrs. Fairchild, that caused Emma more difficulty with her family.

"She may think she is important now," Miss Harper stated with a daggers-drawn stare at Emma, "but you will notice she has not yet appeared at Almack's."

Emma, better able to cope with such spite now, turned to Mrs. Fairchild with a smile, only to see a speculative gleam in her eye. "Oh, no, ma'am. You must not even consider it," Emma protested in alarm. "Mama tried to get invitations for my stepsister and was unable to do so."

"Not only was your stepsister not engaged to my son," Mrs. Fairchild said coolly, "but she also did not have your bloodlines. There is nothing wrong with your family. Your father made a poor choice for a second wife, but that cannot be laid at your feet."

"Truly, Mrs. Fairchild, I do not—"

"We will see, child. Do not grow alarmed," Mrs. Fairchild said, her eyes searching the ballroom.

Emma said nothing else, knowing it would be useless. She had discovered both mother and son had that steel resolve that rolled over any resistance. Putting such thoughts from her mind, she greeted her next partner charmingly and moved onto the dance floor.

Mrs. Fairchild spotted the one person she wanted to find. Lady Sefton, the kindest of the patronesses of Almack's, was chatting with a friend across the room. Without haste, she made her way around the room to greet her old friend.

Two days later, Emma was not really surprised to discover a voucher for Almack's in her morning mail. The rueful smile on her face drew her stepmother's attention.

"What is that?"

Emma looked up in surprise. She had forgotten her stepmother's presence. "J-just a note from Mrs.—"

Without waiting for her to finish, Mrs. Chadwell leaned over the table, narrowly avoiding dipping a ruffle into her tea, and snatched the paper from Emma.

"Mama!" Emma protested.

"A mother has the right to examine her daughter's mail," Mrs. Chadwell exclaimed calmly. Her calm flew out the window when she read the voucher. "Almack's! You have received a voucher for Almack's? And you were not going to tell me? How ungrateful can you be? I bring you to town, dress you fashionably, snare a rich husband for you, and you intended to hide such a thing from your own dear mother?"

Emma closed her eyes and silently struggled to hold back the words that wanted out.

"I cannot believe that you would do such a thing!" Short of breath from such ravings, Mrs. Chadwell paused, and Emma reached for her voucher.

"No! No, no, child. We must plan this event. I will choose your gown and, of course, my own, and we will—"

"The voucher is only for me, Mama."

Emma's quiet statement brought Mrs. Chadwell to an abrupt halt. She stared at the voucher again. The scream that issued from her lips when her eyes confirmed Emma's words brought the butler running.

"Get out! Get out, you idiot!" she yelled at the butler. Rage radiated from her eyes, and her face flushed with hot blood. When the door closed behind the butler, she turned her fire on her stepdaughter. "I should've known, you ungrateful wretch! When have you ever cared about me or mine! Well, you shan't go! I'll not have you lording it over the *ton* when they would not let your dear, sweet sister enter those damned doors!"

It was a sign of Mrs. Chadwell's loss of control that she would utter a blasphemy. Emma, in spite of her lack of affection for the woman, felt pity. Her stepmother had tried so hard to become fashionable, but Society had never accepted her as one of them.

"You will not go! I'll not allow it. You will only enter Almack's when your brother and I are by your side. And so you shall tell Mrs. Fairchild!"

"Mrs. Fairchild cannot obtain vouchers for you and Charlie, Mama. You know how difficult it is to—"

"She got one for you, didn't she? If she wants you at Almack's, she must include the rest of your family, and you just tell her that!" Mrs. Chadwell jumped up from the table and bustled from the room, anger her driving force.

Emma slumped back in her chair. What a bumble bath. She had no desire to attend Almack's, but would do so to please Mrs. Fairchild. Now, even that would be impossible. She could not tell Mrs. Fairchild of her stepmother's reaction. It would be too humiliating. She must determine some way out.

After long contemplation, Emma wrote two notes. For some reason, Mr. Fairchild seemed much the easier of the two to explain the difficulty to. Perhaps because he cared nothing about her, Emma admitted glumly. Shaking her head, she dismissed such foolish thoughts. The man had been honest with her. She must not expect more.

═ 12 ═

MRS. FAIRCHILD THOUGHT nothing of it when Emma excused herself from another shopping expedition, pleading her mother's need of her assistance. After all, even if the woman showed no concern for her daughter, she was planning a wedding for her beloved son. It was just as well that Miss Stokie's mother was not living, because Mrs. Fairchild felt sure Mrs. Chadwell would have taken charge anyway.

Mr. Fairchild, on the other hand, was surprised, and not a little put out, to receive a request for a ride in the park from Emma. He thought she understood he did not have the time to wait on her hand and foot.

His irritable mood was visible in his face when he arrived on her doorstep, and Emma's heart sank. Only the thought of his mother kept her from retreating.

The silence between the two of them as Mr. Fairchild negotiated the streets of London reminded Emma of their first carriage ride. So much had occurred since then, and yet Mr. Fairchild's mood did not seem much improved.

As soon as they entered the park, Emma said, "I apologise for impinging on your time, sir, but I—I have a problem and I do not know how to solve it."

Ashamed that his impatience had shown, Mr. Fairchild eased the pace of his horses and turned to his fiancée. "If I can be of assistance, I am at your service, Emma."

With a deep breath, she explained, "Your mother has obtained a voucher for Almack's for me. It is most considerate of her, but—but my stepmother could not do so when her daughter came out and—and she is much upset that I am to attend and she may not accompany me."

Mr. Fairchild understood the difficulty at once. He knew even the kindest of patronesses would not admit Mrs. Chadwell. "Emma, I believe it would be, uh, difficult for my mother to make that possible."

An unexpected chuckle escaped his companion. "Tactfully put, Richard. I did not mean I expected such heroics from your mother." She looked up at him, her brown eyes earnest. "I am seeking the best way to explain to your mother that I cannot attend. She seemed to have her heart set on it, and I do not want to disappoint her."

Richard stared down into those brown eyes and was reminded once again how wisely he had chosen his bride. Her love and concern for his child and his mother were more than he had expected.

"Richard?"

Brought to attention, Mr. Fairchild hastily remembered that he himself must keep his distance from such emotions. After all, he refused to forfeit his freedom. "I will inform her," he replied brusquely.

They rode in silence for several minutes before Emma asked quietly, "Have I offended you, Richard? Truly, I did not intend to do so."

"Of course not," he replied, surprised. He had not meant to allow his withdrawal to be so evident. After all, while love might be foreign to their marriage, there was no reason friendship could not be allowed. Especially with such a reasonable female.

Unconvinced, Emma added, "We may return home now. I know you have many demands upon your time."

Richard smiled down at his companion. "Nonsense. It is time I take a break from my work. It is a delightful day, and I have a delightful companion. I believe I should take advantage of such a fortuitous situation."

After taking Emma home, Richard entered his town house in a happier frame of mind than when he had left it. The hour in the park with his fiancée had proved delightful, revealing her wry sense of humour that brought a chuckle to his lips in memory.

His mother, descending the stairs, was surprised to discover her son outside of his office, much less with a smile on his face.

"Richard! I thought you were planning to work all day."

With a grin at his mother's surprise, Richard replied, "I had such plans, Mother, but Emma interrupted them."

"Emma? I thought she was needed by her mother this morning."

Richard noted his mother's stiffened features. "Do not be offended, Mother. If you will come to the library, I will explain."

"That is not necessary, Richard. What you and Emma choose to do has nothing to do with me."

"You know that is not true, and you will understand Emma's actions in a few moments," he assured her, extending his hand to urge her down the stairs.

As Mr. Fairchild had promised, Emma was restored to his mother's good opinion shortly thereafter.

"Oh, that poor child. I'm sure that woman has made her life miserable. I foolishly thought I would be helping Emma, and instead I have hurt her."

"Now, Mother, you cannot be blamed for that woman's behaviour. The question is, what shall we do now? Is it essential to your happiness that Emma attend Almack's?"

"Heavens, no. I only obtained the voucher because I wanted *everyone* to know that she has the approval of the *ton*," Mrs. Fairchild said emphatically.

Though he was curious about the emphasis of his mother's statement, Mr. Fairchild only said, "I'm sure everyone knows that."

His mother eyed him speculatively before saying, "They will believe it more readily if you are occasionally in attendance upon us." She raised her hand as he opened his mouth to protest. "I know you have much with which to deal, but I will not have you slight Emma by never appearing with her in the evenings."

"No, of course not, Mother," he promised. When his mother left the library, he contemplated parading around the city in the evenings accompanied by his mother and his fiancée. Those had not exactly been his intentions when he set this curious plan in motion. Remembrance of his drive with Emma consoled him, however. At least he had chosen a rational young woman. He would not mind spending a few evenings with his new friend.

Thus, the pattern of their evenings was set. Mrs. Fairchild requested Emma's company to various social events, though she seldom included Emma's stepmother in the invitations, explaining that she wanted to take Emma off Mrs. Chadwell's hands since she was so busy with her son and his future bride.

Sometimes Mr. Fairchild escorted the two ladies, but at other times, they went alone or were escorted by friends of Mrs. Fairchild. Mrs. Harris, Deborah, and Lord Atherton would meet them at the evening's entertainment, and Emma was surrounded by a small circle of friends that was ever growing.

How different from her first few weeks on the town. She had much to be grateful for, and she attempted to express her appreciation several times to Mrs. Fairchild, but that lady swept her gratitude aside, informing her she was the one who should be grateful, not Emma.

Part of Emma's content stemmed from the fact that her family had given up their scheme of rushing her wedding in order to have her brother in funds. Charlie had sold his phaeton and most of his horses, and, since no further complaints had been made, Emma assumed he had received enough to finance his courtship.

Also, since Emma had not entered those hallowed doors of Almack's, her stepmother had almost forgiven her receiving a voucher. Mrs. Fairchild's understanding had deepened the friendship that existed between her and her daughter-in-law-elect, and even Mr. Fairchild seemed to be happier with his decision.

Only a week before her brother's wedding, Emma attended a soirée at Lady Butterworth's with Mrs. Fairchild and the Harrises, accompanied by Lord Atherton. Mr. Fairchild had promised to drop in later. It was a pleasant evening, and Emma relaxed, prepared to enjoy herself.

Mrs. Fairchild introduced Emma to several new people, but one stood out among the rest. His name was Jonathan Westcott, a quiet, tall gentleman who seemed slightly lost in the glittering social world. The shyness in his eyes reminded Emma strongly of herself, and she could not resist reaching out to him to ease his introduction to the *ton*.

"Is this your first visit to London, Mr. Westcott?" she asked gently.

"No, Miss . . . uh, Miss Chadwell. I visited it once before when I was very young."

"You are not so ancient now, Mr. Westcott."

"Well, ma'am, I am feeling my age this evening. Everything seems to have changed a great deal."

"I am sure you will grow more comfortable soon, Mr. Westcott."

The man shook his head, a rueful grin on his face. "I fear you are mistaken, young lady. I believe I belong in the country."

"As do I. I much prefer it to the city, but I have managed to grow more comfortable here."

"You? In the country? But you are so . . . so elegant, Miss Chadwell. I cannot imagine you in the country. That is, unless you mean the country where you remain in the house, never venturing outdoors."

"You misjudge me, sir," Emma returned with a smile. "I managed my brother's estate for a number of years, and enjoy discussion of crops and horses much more than . . . than the latest *on dit*."

Mr. Westcott wasted no time testing the young lady's boast and discovered, much to his surprise, that she had told the truth. Feeling he had found a lifeline in the fast moving glitter of the *ton*, he remained by her side most of the evening.

Mr. Fairchild did not appear that evening, but because of Mr. Westcott's attentiveness, Emma scarcely noticed, though she did occasionally search for an auburn head among the tall men present.

In the carriage returning home, Mrs. Fairchild hesitantly

spoke to her future daughter-in-law. "Emma, dear, I know we are not yet related, but . . . but may I offer you some advice? If you do not mind?"

"Of course I do not mind, Mrs. Fairchild. What is it?"

"Dear, Mr. Westcott is a very nice man, but you are to be married shortly. His attentiveness to you caused some talk this evening."

"Surely you are teasing, Mrs. Fairchild? We did not do more than discuss farming."

"Yes, I know," Mrs. Fairchild said with a chuckle. "I did not mean to imply I thought you might betray Richard, dear, but others could not know the subject of your discussions. And they do know it is rumoured that Mr. Westcott came to town to seek a wife. You see, his mother died last year, and he has no one to keep house for him now. It is said he is ready to set up his nursery."

"Oh! I did not know."

Mrs. Fairchild leaned forward to press Emma's hand. "I know you will do the right thing, Emma. I just thought you should know what is being said."

"I'm sorry, Mrs. Fairchild, if I caused you any worry. I am happier now than I have ever been, and I would do nothing to disturb you. I will take care in the future."

"I felt sure you would, child. You are such a dear."

The next evening, Emma again attended a social event with Mrs. Fairchild, but this time Mr. Fairchild was in attendance, escorting them to a ball at Mrs. Featherstone's. Emma felt particularly well turned out, her dress a gift from Mrs. Fairchild in a primrose yellow that flattered her eyes and made her complexion glow. Nancy had worked a particularly intricate knot on top of her head and woven daisies through it, making many think of spring when Emma came into view.

Before they left the carriage, Mrs. Fairchild, who had known the dress Emma would wear, offered her a necklace and bracelet of yellow topaz to complement her gown.

"Oh, no! Mrs. Fairchild, you mustn't—"

"And why not? It goes very well with your gown."

"But, ma'am, I cannot accept such an expensive gift. You have already purchased more gowns than I should have allowed. To take this also would be too much."

"Pooh! They are only topazes, not yellow diamonds. They are not that expensive, are they, Richard?"

Mr. Fairchild was pleased with Emma that evening, but he had given little thought to the normal rudiments of a courtship, such as gifts. Now he frowned at his mother, feeling he had been found lacking somehow. "They are very nice, Mother."

"That is not what I asked you, Richard. Topazes are not an expensive gift, and as we are to be related, it is perfectly all right for Emma to accept them, is it not?"

"Yes, that is true, Mother. Do you not have jewels of your own, Emma?"

Feeling Mr. Fairchild was chastising her for making his mother feel the need to buy her jewellery, Emma stiffened and said formally, "Only an aquamarine drop given me by my father, but I am quite content as I am. I thank you, ma'am, for wanting to give me such a lovely gift, but I must not accept."

Rather than blaming Emma for her response, Mrs. Fairchild looked at her only child. "You are not of much assistance, I must say, Richard. Now you have made the child feel guilty for not having jewellery, and it is certainly not her fault."

"I did no such thing. If that is how Emma interpreted my remarks, then she is at fault."

Emma looked away, refusing to respond to his words.

"Well, that is certainly how you made her feel. Am I also at fault for thinking you did so?"

Not used to being attacked by his mother, Mr. Fairchild said defensively, "I did not intend that, Mother. Certainly I would not expect Emma to have a large selection of jewels, but most young women have a string of pearls or something."

"And most young women who are engaged to someone as rich as you would be wearing a magnificent engagement ring, but I have seen nothing on her fingers. Have you given one to her and she has refused to wear it?"

"Please!" Emma cried, embarrassed by their discussion.

"One moment, Emma," Mr. Fairchild said authoritatively. "Mother, the reason I did not offer Emma a ring is that we retreated to the country before I could make arrangements for one suitable to the occasion."

"Oh? Then I suppose you have visited a jeweller since our return? After all, you must also purchase a wedding ring for her. And most young women expect presents prior to the wedding. Just because Emma does not insist on such things, does not mean you can slight her."

"I had no intention of slighting her! I just . . . everything happened so quickly."

"Mrs. Fairchild, please. It is of no consequence. I do not expect—"

"But *I* do, child. You are very dear to me, and I will not have the *ton* making sport about the way Richard is treating you."

"What are you talking about?" Mr. Fairchild said sharply.

"Have you not heard the whispers?"

"No, and I would appreciate your telling me what is being said."

Emma blushed painfully. She had heard whispers, and Deborah had hesitantly asked her several questions that had further informed her. She knew the *ton* realised the kind of marriage offer she had received. They did not blame her for accepting. That was a way of life in Society. But they blamed her lack of presence and beauty for her not demanding that Mr. Fairchild keep up the pretences.

But though she had heard and understood what was being said, she had said nothing to Mr. Fairchild. He had explained what kind of marriage he desired, and she had agreed to it. With the code of honour taught to her by her father, she would not complain. And she certainly had no desire to go back on her agreement.

"They are saying that you proposed marriage to Emma because you wanted a woman to care for your child, and that you care nothing for her."

His mother's blunt reply hit painfully close to home. Mr. Fairchild cast one brief glance on Emma's composed face before he turned back to his mother.

"I have been in attendance some evenings. You know I have business interests that require my attention."

"Yes, but it is not enough." She held up her hand to stop his protest. "I know. I thought it might do, but there have been whispers."

"Mother, you do not understand."

"I understand all too well, son. But while I understand, even if I don't approve your reasons for marriage, there is no excuse for bruiting it all over the *ton*. No one, least of all Emma, deserves the scorn she has received from the proud beauties who tried to entrap you."

"Emma, my apologies," Mr. Fairchild said stiffly. "I did not mean—"

"Please, your mother is exaggerating," Emma assured him quietly. "I did not expect gifts, Richard. I understand the nature of your proposal."

Her acceptance of his behaviour, his casual treatment of Emma since their return to town, made it seem even worse. He felt considerable guilt at causing the young lady opposite him any distress. She had already given him a great deal in regard to his daughter.

Mrs. Fairchild looked at her son impatiently. He seemed struck dumb by their conversation. She reached over to take Emma's hand. "Child, take the necklace and bracelet. They truly are paltry items, but perhaps they will express my love for you. It would mean a lot to me if you would do so."

Emma, made uneasy by Mr. Fairchild's silence, squeezed the hand of the woman she now loved more than any member of her own family. With a sideways look at her fiancé, she said, "All right." Leaning forward, she allowed Mrs. Fairchild to fasten the catch of the necklace. Then Emma put the bracelet in place while Mr. Fairchild watched. But Emma only looked at the older woman when she asked, "How do they look?"

"Stunning, child, as do you. You grow more elegant every day."

Unable to resist the kindness that seemed to always flow from this woman, Emma leaned forward and hugged her, whispering her gratitude in her ear.

Mr. Fairchild watched the pair with a frown on his face. It behooved him to rectify his mistakes, beginning with the evening ahead of him. And tomorrow, he would visit the jeweller.

He had not intended to involve himself too much in the demands of courtship, but his mother was correct. He should not leave Emma to the mercy of the debutantes who had been snubbed by his proposal to her.

Mr. Fairchild called on Emma the next day to take her for another ride in the park. As had become Mrs. Chadwell's custom, she no longer bothered to be present on those occasions.

Emma, dressed in a peach muslin gown that was reflected in her cheeks, greeted Richard and picked up the matching parasol, ready to depart.

"One moment, Emma. While we are alone, there is something I have for you."

Turning, wide-eyed, Emma wanted to die when he pulled forth a small box. While she would have loved a gift presented with his love, she had come to realise that expensive baubles meant nothing to her without it.

Numbly shaking her head, she took a step backwards.

"Emma, I will not be rebuked by my mother for unchivalrous behaviour towards you again. Besides, you should have an engagement ring. And there is no question but that you must have a wedding ring. Otherwise, Melissa might not believe that you are her mother," he teased, hoping to ease the strain between them.

"Truly, sir, it is not necessary. Melissa will not—"

He stepped to her side and carried her hand to his lips. "Perhaps not, but I will. I am not handling this well, my dear, but I *want* to give you this ring." He paused to open the box, and Emma gasped. "Not because of my mother, but as a sign of our pledge to each other."

She stared at the yellow diamond surrounded by white ones. It was the most beautiful ring she'd ever seen. When he took her hand and slid the ring on her finger, she made no protest. Indeed, she wasn't sure she could speak, such was her confusion.

"I also purchased a small gift to celebrate the occasion," he added.

Her brown eyes flashed up to his. "But I will not be able to give you a gift, Richard. It is not fair that . . ."

Used to women who demanded fabulous jewels for the slightest of reasons, Mr. Fairchild smiled at Emma's idea of justice. "Emma, my love, it is the gentleman's prerogative to do so."

"But . . ."

He opened a larger box to reveal a lustrous string of pearls with a diamond clasp. "Hush, my dear. These are for you to wear on our wedding day."

Tears filled her eyes and she quickly turned from him, hoping to hide her emotions. His large hands settled on her shoulders and turned her to face him.

"Do not cry, Emma. Take the pearls up to your chamber, and it might be wise to hide them from your stepmother," he added apologetically.

Emma nodded without speaking and whisked herself from the room. She returned after a few minutes, composed, and accompanied him to his carriage.

They passed the time driving to the park with mundane conversation, but Emma kept staring at the ring on her finger.

When Mr. Fairchild caught her doing so, she rushed into speech. "Your mother received a letter from Mrs. Quigley with a drawing from Melissa yesterday."

"Do you miss her?"

"Oh, yes. And Fairchild House and everyone there. You are fortunate to have such an estate."

"Fortunate? I worked very hard and suffered the climate in India in order to have Fairchild House."

"You have never spoken of your sojourn in India. Will you tell me about it?"

Mr. Fairchild grinned. "I was afraid I would bore you. But if you are interested, I will do so."

"I would enjoy it, sir." Her gaze returned to the ring. "I am afraid my ring must've cost you many more hours in such difficult circumstances."

"The labor has already been done. And you must stop protesting whatever I do. It does not bode well for our marriage that you do not allow me authority over you." His grin allowed Emma to relax.

"Did the first Mrs. Fairchild—"

"We will not discuss my first wife," Mr. Fairchild said frostily, causing Emma to drop her head.

Her immediate retreat caused a feeling of guilt to invade his anger, and as soon as they had entered the paths of Hyde Park, he lifted her hand and carried it to his lips.

"Forgive me. I did not mean to growl at you. Now, would you truly like to hear about life in India?"

Emma recognised a peace offering when she saw one and swiftly assured him of her interest.

= 13 =

WHEN EMMA ARRIVED at the next ball sporting the canary-yellow diamond, she gained new respect among the members of the *ton*. In addition, she was accompanied by Richard, and they were seen dancing together several times.

For Mr. Fairchild, who had expected such duty to be incredibly boring, the evening was an enlightenment. There was such a contrast between Emma and the other young women, like Miss Harper, that he found it a pleasure. She made no demands upon him, and when he offered her gallant compliments, she not only did not beg for more but turned the conversation to matters of interest to both of them.

Emma had been fascinated by his tales of India, and he enjoyed such an intelligent listener. Her questions about his life there demonstrated her interest. When he, in turn, asked about her years as manager of her brother's estate, she willingly explained the growth of her interest and experience. He enjoyed the dry humour he had earlier discovered in his fiancée.

There had been no conversation in his first marriage. They had either argued or he had flattered and cajoled the spoilt young lady. He did not know a young woman could be such a sensible and pleasant companion as Emma. Every hour spent in her company gave him greater satisfaction in his choice of bride. There was no question now, in Mr. Fairchild's mind, whether their marriage would be real. Of course, that did not mean he would be tied down to a staid life in the country. Emma would have to understand that he must have his freedom.

Emma, having already discovered Mr. Fairchild's attractiveness, was fast becoming addicted to his presence. She found her eyes searching the room when he was not close by, and she waited breathlessly for his arrival each day to take her for a drive. Though she realised she was asking for heartache, she found herself incapable of doing otherwise.

"You are looking particularly elegant this evening, Emma," Mr. Fairchild whispered in her ear as he swung her around the room in an energetic waltz.

"Thank you, Richard. Have you seen Deborah and James this evening?"

"No. Did you need to communicate with them?"

"Deborah asked if we would like to accompany them on a picnic out into the country tomorrow, and I need to tell her I cannot."

"But you have not even asked me. I think I would like to go on a picnic."

Emma smiled regretfully. "Then you must accompany them, sir, but I cannot. My mother demands my presence at a tea for Miss Stokie tomorrow afternoon."

"Ah, the infamous Miss Stokie. You have met her?"

Mr. Fairchild watched the corners of her mouth quiver with repressed humour and discovered a sudden urge to place a kiss just there. Surprised, he drew back and stared at the young lady.

"Yes, I . . . What is the matter, Richard?"

"The matter? Nothing. Nothing is the matter. What were you saying?"

"I met Miss Stokie several days ago. She is . . . she is an interesting person."

"I am looking forward to meeting the intrepid young woman."

"Intrepid?"

"Forgive me, my dear, but anyone who would take on your brother must be considered either intrepid or a lunatic. He is young and reckless."

"I quite agree with you, though, as he is my brother, I should not."

"I will never betray you," Mr. Fairchild assured her, pulling her slightly closer to him as he swung her about the room.

Emma stared up at his handsome face, admiration in her eyes, "No . . . I know I can trust you, Richard."

"Mother said you had written to Melissa."

"Yes, for Mrs. Quigley to read to her. I'm afraid she is becoming most impatient for us to return."

"Not us, my dear Emma, but you."

"She is looking forward to your return, also, Richard, now that she feels she knows you. After all, a little girl needs her father."

"Now, Emma. You know I do not know anything about children. You are the one who is supposed to take care of Melissa."

Emma's chin dropped at the reminder of her role in this marriage. Far too often lately, she had been indulging in fantasy.

"Emma?" Mr. Fairchild questioned, surprised at her reaction. However, he received no reply as the music ended, making it acceptable for his partner to pull away from him. He offered her his arm and escorted her from the floor, but he could think of nothing to say with others passing so closely to them, some even stopping to greet them.

When he delivered Emma back to his mother's side, there was no question of a private conversation. His only opportunity would be during another dance. He could then ask her to sit with him. "May I have another dance later, Emma?" he asked casually.

"No, I'm sorry, Richard, but my card is full."

"Surely as your intended husband I am entitled to another dance if I desire it?"

Emma was both relieved and disappointed to deny him, but she said firmly, "I am sorry, but you only selected two dances, Richard, and the others are promised." The arrival of her next partner pinpointed her reply, and Richard strolled away with an irritated expression on his face.

Emma took the floor with her next partner, but her thoughts were with Mr. Fairchild. She rebuked herself for her foolishness in believing that he might care about her. She should be grateful that she was going to have such a wonderful home and new family without expecting her husband to . . . to love her, she reminded herself with a sigh.

"Are you fatigued, Miss Chadwell?" her partner asked.

Emma smiled up at him apologetically. "No, of course not, Mr. Anglesly. I am sorry. I'm afraid I was thinking about a . . . a problem I have to solve."

"If I may serve you . . ."

"Oh, goodness no, sir, but I appreciate your kind offer. You drive a wonderful pair of bays, do you not? I believe I saw you in Hyde Park the other morning."

"Yes, I do. They are a magnificent pair, ma'am. Raring to go. I'm going to race them to Brighton against my friend Robinson's grays next week."

"My! How exciting! I do hope . . ." Emma continued the topic throughout the dance, putting her problems from her mind and making the young gentleman feel that Mr. Fairchild was a very lucky man. Mr. Fairchild, leaning against a garlanded pillar, did not feel quite so lucky as he watched Emma enchant the young man. It was true she did not flirt like the other young women, but she made one feel comfortable. And when she smiled, it was as if a lantern had been lit inside her, exuding warmth.

Mr. Fairchild thought back to the first time he had set eyes on Miss Chadwell, sitting hunched over in those overpowering ruffles and frizzy hair, unknown to anyone. Because of him, she was fast becoming the toast of the Season, and he could not even have a third dance if he wanted it.

In disgust, he abandoned his observation post and headed to the card room. He would be unable to have a private discussion with Emma until the next morning when he called upon her for their usual morning drive. He was determined to put all thought of her from his mind until then.

After Mr. Fairchild departed for cards, Mr. Westcott came to claim his partner. Emma had seen him once in the park since they had spent the evening talking, but Mrs. Fairchild's warning had made her feel awkward and she had spoken only to him in passing. Now she joined him on the floor on her guard. She must do nothing to cause tongues to wag.

"Miss Fairchild, I had hoped to see you before now, but when I called at your home, you were not in."

"My brother's wedding is rapidly approaching, Mr. Westcott, shortly followed by my own, and there is much to do."

Emma ignored the fallen face of her partner and his hesitation in the dance. She had wanted to be sure he understood her situation before their acquaintance grew any greater.

"I . . . see. I did not know . . . I was not aware that I should wish you happy, Miss Chadwell. Though I am not surprised that you are to be married. You are such a charming companion, I am sure you have been much in demand."

"Thank you, Mr. Westcott. My engagement is fairly recent, but the notices have appeared in the paper."

"I only just arrived in London. Perhaps they appeared before my arrival. Who is the lucky man?"

"Mr. Fairchild."

"Ah . . . the young man who made his fortune in India. He caused quite a stir upon his return, did he not? Come to think of it, I thought he married one of the belles of the Season."

"Yes, he did, but she died a few years ago."

"Ah. I had thought . . . that is, after our enjoyable coze the other evening, I had even considered—"

"Please, Mr. Westcott, I do not believe you should . . ."

"No, you are quite right. But, Miss Chadwell, should you ever . . . should you decide not to marry Mr. Fairchild for any reason, please know that I would be honoured if you would . . ."

Emma's cheeks were flaming as they circled the room, and she strove for greater control. "Thank you. The weather has been unseasonably warm, has it not, Mr. Westcott?"

The man grimaced at her conversational gambit but did not pursue his earlier topic.

Mr. Fairchild had stayed only a few minutes in the card room, looking over a friend's shoulder, but a restlessness he could not explain drove him back into the ballroom. He arrived just in time to see Emma dancing in the arms of a stranger who was causing her to blush.

His eyes sharpened as he watched them finish their dance. When he saw them cross the room to his mother, he hurried over to be presented.

"Mother, Emma, it is a pleasant party, is it not? Ah, I do not believe I know your partner, Emma."

Emma recognized immediately a tone in his voice that did not bode well for the introduction, but she offered it calmly. "Richard, may I present Mr. Westcott? Mr. Westcott, Mr. Fairchild."

"Congratulations, Fairchild," Mr. Westcott said as he shook hands with the other man. "You are a lucky fellow to be marrying Miss Chadwell."

"Yes, I am, am I not?" Mr. Fairchild returned arrogantly with a grim smile on his face.

"Richard!" his mother chided. "That was most ungracious of you. Mr. Westcott, I believe I knew your mother. I was sorry to hear of her demise." Mrs. Fairchild drew the man away from the engaged couple with questions about his family.

"And what was Mr. Westcott saying to you to cause such a blush upon your cheeks?"

Emma fought to control the tide of warmth that returned to her face as she met his eyes levelly. "He was paying me some very pretty compliments."

"You do not blush like that when I pay you compliments."

"You are supposed to pay me compliments, Richard. We are engaged."

"I know we are engaged, young lady, but I wanted to be sure you know it also."

"You sound like a dog worrying over a bone he has already buried, Richard. Do not be silly."

Her calm answer did not soothe Mr. Fairchild's rising anger. "I will thank you not to make a spectacle of yourself now that you are engaged to me. I do not care for talk about us."

Emma's features stiffened as she sharply drew in her breath. "I have done nothing to cause talk! How dare you say such a thing!"

"Children, please, if you must argue, can you not do so more privately?" Mrs. Fairchild asked, returning to their side.

"I have no need to argue with Mr. Fairchild," Emma assured the older lady righteously. "However, I will not stand by and allow him to question my behaviour when it has been exemplary."

"I do not call it exemplary to be cavorting on the dance floor with that man, blushing blood red!"

"Richard, really!" his mother exclaimed. "You sound as if you are jealous of Mr. Westcott. They met only the other evening. Just because he . . . appreciates Emma's company does not mean you have cause for jealousy. After all, she is wearing your ring."

"I am not jealous!" Mr. Fairchild seethed, feeling set upon by his own mother.

"Of course not, dear," she returned, patting his arm carelessly. "Oh, look, there are James and Deborah trying to gain your attention. Aren't they a handsome couple?"

There was no time for any further comments before the arrival of the other couple, but Mr. Fairchild intended to take up the matter with Emma the next day.

Early the next morning, Emma came to the conclusion that it would be best if she were not available for a ride in the park with Mr. Fairchild that day. One of her reasons was to avoid any more questions regarding Mr. Westcott. She had done nothing wrong, but she wasn't sure she could convince Richard.

The other reason had to do with her own emotions. She was enjoying her engagement too much lately, letting herself believe it was a love match. It was time for her to face the truth. And she found that difficult to do in Mr. Fairchild's presence.

She composed a very short and sedate note, explaining her mother's need for her this morning and begging to be excused. She knew Mr. Fairchild would not take well to being thwarted in his desire to question her, but perhaps he would forget his concerns if they were postponed.

* * *

Mr. Fairchild was irritated when the note was delivered to him at his breakfast table. And he had no intention of forgetting his questions of the evening before. However, he decided it might be more informative if he discovered what he could about Mr. Westcott. To that end, he proceeded to his club and settled himself with a newspaper in the reading room.

It was not long before James strolled in accompanied by several other friends, and Richard hailed them. The three men willingly joined Mr. Fairchild and talked desultorily for a few minutes before he asked casually, "Anyone here familiar with a Mr. Westcott?"

"Yes, I know Westcott," Lord Hampton said.

"Oh? I met him last night. Seemed a nice fellow."

"Oh, he is, the best of good fellows."

"What brings him to town?" Mr. Fairchild asked.

"His mother died a year ago. Heard he's decided to marry," Lord Hampton replied. " 'Tis why he came to town."

"You mean he has someone in mind?"

"Well, he didn't when he first arrived, but I talked to him several days ago, and he said he had met someone he was rather taken with."

Mr. Fairchild gripped the arms of his chair tightly, but no emotion showed in his voice when he asked, "Oh? Did he say who she is?"

"No, he didn't say. Probably afraid I'd beat him to his quarry."

There was general laughter, as all four knew Lord Hampton was ranked among the confirmed bachelors by the husband-hunting mamas of the *ton*. Mr. Fairchild turned the subject to the latest boxing match, and no more was said about Mr. Westcott until the other two gentlemen excused themselves. Then Lord Atherton turned to his friend. "What was all that about this Mr. Westcott?"

"Hmmm? Oh, I met him last night. I was just curious."

Lord Atherton frowned. "Can't see why he would interest you. He's a nice enough fellow, but rather a staid, country type, you know."

Quite like Emma, who preferred the country to the city, Mr. Fairchild thought, grinding his teeth. He looked up to discover Lord Atherton watching him closely. "You are right, I have no interest in him."

Lord Atherton still looked askance, but he followed Mr. Fairchild's lead when he changed the subject, and Mr. Fairchild filed away the information. He was determined to protect what was his own from all comers.

Emma, dressed in one of her new gowns, attended the reception for Miss Stokie with some misgivings. The guests were a mixture of Miss Stokie's friends and Emma's stepmother's. There were awkward silences and a separation of the guests. While Emma tried to mingle with her future sister-in-law's friends, she felt ill at ease.

She found herself next to Miss Stokie at one point in the afternoon, the first time she had had an opportunity to talk to the young woman. While her looks were not impressive—she was overweight and had a sallow complexion, small eyes, and a pug nose—Emma looked beneath the covering for admirable traits.

"It is a lovely party, Miss Stokie," she began tentatively.

The young lady laughed, a raw sound that split the air. "Nay, Miss Chadwell, no need to pitch such gammon to me. Your ma is happy with all this, but I can see it makes you uncomfortable."

"Truly, Miss Stokie, it is only because I am rather shy. You see, I am used to the country. I have lived at home most of my life."

"Yes, your brother told me. But don't be countin' on camping there after our wedding. I don't hold with family living off me."

Emma blinked rapidly while she took in the young woman's blunt statement. It was not the sentiment that stunned her, since her brother had already told her she no longer would be welcome in her own home. It was the openness with which Miss Stokie spoke. "Why . . . no, Miss Stokie. I am to be married two weeks after your marriage."

"Yes, Mr. Chadwell told me. He also mentioned you were

a little reluctant. I just want to tell you that you'd best stick with the man, because there's no place with us."

Her words grated on Emma's good manners. Icily, she said, "I can assure you, Miss Stokie, I have no intention of living in the same house with you."

"Ah, now I've gone and offended you, and I really didn't mean to. But I believe in plain speaking. Saves grief later. Why, I won't even allow my own pa to plant himself on me. After all, we each have to live our own lives."

Emma stared at the young woman as if she were in a freak show. She had felt sorry for her, knowing her brother to be young and selfish, but now she thought it was quite possible her brother had discovered someone who deserved him as a husband, as incredible as that seemed. She murmured a polite response and returned to her stepmother's side.

Mrs. Chadwell greeted her stepdaughter's return with a satisfied smile. "Did you see that elegant gown Miss Stokie is wearing? Pure silk, it is. It must have cost a fortune! What luck that she accepted your brother. Though, of course, Charlie is such a charmer, I'm not surprised."

Emma stared at the purple silk gown worn by Miss Stokie and wondered again at her stepmother's taste. The gown was overloaded with ruffles and lace and only made the young woman look larger than she was. "Yes, Mama," she agreed quietly, wishing the afternoon would soon be over.

"Yes, I am a lucky woman. Why, even you, Emma, though you have disappointed me in the past, are doing me proud. Mr. Fairchild is a good catch. Of course, it is not as romantic as Aurora's marriage, but since her husband is such a spendthrift, I would even have to consider your marriage better than Aurora's." Mrs. Chadwell gave a congratulatory smile to her stepdaughter and continued, "In three weeks, all my children will be well married, and I shall spend my days visiting them, giving them the benefit of my wisdom and enjoying my grandchildren. What a lucky woman I am!"

Emma thought about Miss Stokie's attitude towards family and knew her stepmother was going to be disappointed.

Mrs. Chadwell, in her satisfaction, reached over and patted Emma's hand. "I know you have had a difficult time this Season, Emma, and many's the time you have disappointed me, but as Mr. Shakespeare said, 'All's well that ends well.' Don't you agree?"

"I suppose, Mama. But . . ."—she could not allow her stepmother to walk blindly into Miss Stokie's solid wall of rejection—"but sometimes newlyweds do not always . . . are not always ready for guests."

Mrs. Chadwell looked with icy coldness down her nose at her stepdaughter. "If you are trying to tell me I shall not be welcome at Fairchild House, just save your breath, young lady. You would be the last on my list to visit, anyway. After all, Aurora and Charlie have always given me such pleasure, while you . . ."

Emma shut out her stepmother's harangue. So much for her attempt at kindness. Mrs. Chadwell thought she had been warning her away from Fairchild House, and while that had not been her intent, she would not say anything now.

$== 14 ==$

EMMA PREPARED FOR the evening's entertainment with a mixture of anticipation and dread. She was eager to see Richard again, having missed their usual ride that morning, but she feared the power of his attraction to her. She must not forget that he was marrying her only to provide Melissa with a mother.

Also, she was to begin the evening in the company of her stepmother and brother and his future wife. They were all attending the same ball at Mrs. Witherspoon's. It would be Miss Stokie's first venture into the *ton*, and Emma would have preferred not to observe their reaction.

One gown Mrs. Fairchild had purchased for her had not yet been worn. Emma had saved it for a very special occasion. And since she felt the need to look her best this evening, she chose that gown. Its burnished gold silk gave a warm glow to her skin and enhanced her large brown eyes. Adorned with her topaz set and her engagement ring, she appeared as a golden fairy.

Facing herself in the mirror, Emma tugged at the bodice of the gown. She had not remembered its being so low cut.

"Nay, Miss Emma, you'll spoil the pretty gown. Leave't alone. You've nothing to be ashamed of. A fine figure of a woman, you are."

"Thank you, Nancy," Emma grimaced, "but I'd rather not expose myself to strangers."

"Why, this is not half as revealing as some wear. You look fine, Miss Emma. Mr. Fairchild will be pleased."

"I hope so. I don't think he was too happy with me when last we parted."

"There be nothing wrong?" Nancy asked in hasty concern.

"No, I don't think so. He wanted to ask me about someone, and . . . and I avoided his questions."

"Well, it will make me that happy when we move to Fairchild House, I don't mind tellin' you, Miss Emma. You were so happy there."

"Yes." Emma sighed. With a shake of her head, she smiled at her maid. "It won't be long now, Nancy."

The old maid gave Emma a hug before she swiftly backed away and smoothed her gown. "You'll make him want to hurry the day, the way you look tonight, lovey."

By the time Emma arrived at the ball, she already had a splitting headache. Her brother's silence, her stepmother's ignoring her existence, her future sister-in-law's raucous voice and incredibly tasteless gown, all added to the difficulty of the day, and Emma was exhausted before she began.

While they waited in line to be presented to their hostess, Emma scanned the few people she could see. Though she was looking for her fiancé or his mother, she could not help observing Society's reaction to Miss Stokie. It did not bode for a pleasant evening.

After she greeted her hostess, the poor woman scarcely noticing her when her eyes fell on Miss Stokie behind her, Emma moved into the ballroom, not waiting for her family. *I am a coward*, she told herself reproachfully, but even at her worst, she had not rivalled Miss Stokie as a figure of fun.

The misguided young woman had dressed in wide green and silver stripes that only magnified her large size. The bodice was heavily ruffled but cut revealingly low, and it was countered by an enormous emerald necklace and earrings. Her hair was piled so high that it appeared in danger of toppling at any moment. She had dressed it with four green plumes, one of which refused to remain upright, dangling by her left ear.

It was all Emma could do not to laugh in her face, as

some of the *ton* were already doing. She knew from past experience how cruel they could be, and she had resolved not to add to the young lady's pain, in spite of her earlier conversation with her.

"Emma, dear, here you are. I was beginning to wonder if you were coming. My, don't you look stunning this evening!"

"Oh! Mrs. Fairchild, I am so glad to see you," Emma said as she took the older woman's hands. "I . . . that is, my family is with me. Would you care to have Miss Stokie presented to you?"

Mrs. Fairchild looked dubiously in that young lady's direction and wished she had a choice. But Mrs. Chadwell was bearing down upon them with her son and his intended in tow.

"Yes, of course, dear. Good evening, Mrs. Chadwell. How nice to see you again."

"And you, Mrs. Fairchild. Allow me to present my new daughter to you. This is Miss Mary Stokie, my son's promised wife. Mary, this is Mrs. Fairchild, Emma's future mama-in-law."

"How d'do?" Miss Stokie said genially, preening her green feathers.

"How do you do, Miss Stokie. I am pleased to make your acquaintance."

"My pa said everyone would be when they got a whiff of his fortune. That's why I wore my emeralds this evening. Didn't want to leave anyone in doubt."

"They . . . they are certainly magnificent," Mrs. Fairchild managed to get out while Emma choked beside her.

"Even without your wonderful emeralds," Mrs. Chadwell gushed to Miss Stokie, "they will be delighted to receive you because you are Charlie's future wife. Everyone loves Charlie, you know."

Even allowing for a mother's natural prejudice, that remark was ridiculous, but no one challenged Mrs. Chadwell's assertion. Mrs. Fairchild decided she should remove herself from the trio before she completely lost control.

"Would you excuse Emma, please? I want to introduce

her to some of her future neighbours. Oh, and if you do not mind, we will be delighted to escort Emma home. My son should be arriving shortly."

"Of course, of course. We may go on to several other parties, and Emma would probably prefer to return home. She is not such a social butterfly as I am." Mrs. Chadwell tittered as she dismissed the two other women.

Emma and Mrs. Fairchild walked away without a word until they had reached the other side of the ballroom. Then, very carefully, Emma said, "I want to thank you, ma'am, for your forbearance."

"Oh, Emma . . . I wasn't sure I had such control. I am sorry, my dear, but . . . that woman!"

"Are you referring to my stepmother or my future sister-in-law?" Emma asked dryly.

Mrs. Fairchild chuckled. "You are such a dear, Emma, for not taking offence."

"How could I? I am only grateful you rescued me. I could not have survived several more parties with Miss Stokie."

"She certainly will not blend in with the crowd."

"No. I cannot think she will. Did you say Mr. Fairchild will be arriving later?"

"Yes," Mrs. Fairchild replied. "I came with Katherine and Deborah Harris because he and Lord Atherton had a dinner engagement with an old friend who had lately arrived in London. They promised to join us as soon as possible. Richard seemed particularly eager to see you," she added with satisfaction.

"Only because he wants to question me about Mr. Westcott and I excused myself from our morning drive."

"Oh. Well, that may be the reason, but when he sees you, he is sure to be impressed. I have never seen you look lovelier, my dear."

Emma's response was interrupted by several young men asking to sign her dance card. When Mr. Westcott joined them, Emma made no complaint. It would have drawn attention to both of them, and besides, Mr. Fairchild was not here, and she needed all the friends she could find. Once Miss Stokie had made the rounds, she was not sure anyone other than Mrs. Fairchild would even speak to her.

The evening progressed agonisingly slowly for Emma. Mr. Fairchild had not yet arrived, and she had to endure the whispers racing around the room. Miss Stokie seemed oblivious of the reaction of the *ton* to her presence, but Charles Chadwell and his mother appeared more and more aware of it.

Mr. Chadwell, in fact, wore a ferocious scowl and hung back whenever his mother pushed forward to another introduction. But even Mrs. Chadwell grew more reluctant to do so after several snubs. It was with great relief that Emma saw the three of them take their leave, presumably to go on to other parties.

When Mr. Westcott appeared for his first dance, Emma was grateful to partner someone with whom she could relax and be herself. As they moved across the room, she asked Mr. Westcott questions about his crop rotation, but he answered her randomly.

"Is anything the matter, Mr. Westcott? Have I displeased you? Or is it my family that has caused your distraction?" Emma asked wryly.

"Your family? I'm sorry, I do not know your family, Miss Chadwell."

His response caused Emma to chuckle. "Then something must be of great importance, Mr. Westcott, because everyone else here this evening has maligned my future sister-in-law."

"Oh. You mean the . . . the young woman in the striped gown. She is going to marry your brother?"

"Yes, I'm afraid so."

"Oh. No, that is not the reason. I—I need to talk to you, Miss Chadwell. May I call on you tomorrow?"

"I don't think—that is, I usually drive with Mr. Fairchild in the mornings, and my brother's wedding is so soon."

"Please! I must speak with you. May we sit and talk? There would be nothing improper in that."

His pleading was difficult to resist. And in everyone's presence, she could see nothing wrong with granting him his request. "Yes, if you want, Mr. Westcott."

"Thank you, Miss Chadwell." He said nothing else the rest of the dance, his brow furled in concentration, and Emma grew more concerned each minute.

What could Mr. Westcott want to discuss? She could not imagine what was disturbing him, but she was distracted from pursuing that train of thought when she saw Mr. Fairchild and Lord Atherton arrive.

Her eyes dwelt lovingly on Mr. Fairchild's tall, elegant form, but she also noticed how many other young women took note of his arrival. It was a depressing thought when combined with the fact that after their marriage, she would be left at Fairchild House to care for Melissa and he would return to London. It did not bear thinking about. She put it from her mind and smiled warmly up at Mr. Westcott.

"Ah, there is your mother and Mrs. Harris over by that potted palm. Shall we join them?"

"Yes," Mr. Fairchild agreed absently, his eyes having just discovered the object of his search. He frowned when he realised her partner was Mr. Westcott. Following in Lord Atherton's wake to join the two older ladies, he kept his eyes on Emma and was witness to the warm smile she bestowed on her partner.

"Richard, James, we are so glad you have arrived. We have been most naughty, gossiping. It is good you are here to keep us from behaving badly," Mrs. Harris joked as the two men joined them.

"Gossiping? Have we missed something eventful?" Lord Atherton asked.

"Only the presentation of Miss Stokie to the *ton*," Mrs. Fairchild said. "It was an incredible sight."

"Ah, yes," Mr. Fairchild agreed. "I have seen the young lady. Quite an original, isn't she?"

"You are too kind, my dear boy," Mrs. Harris said. "She is an absolute horror!"

Mrs. Fairchild hid her smile behind her hand before adding, "Thank goodness they moved on to other parties. I am sure it made the evening more enjoyable for Emma. I told her mother we would see her home, Richard."

"Of course, Mother. I would not have it any other way. I have been looking forward to seeing her all day."

"She looks wonderful this evening, does she not?" Mrs. Fairchild asked proudly.

"It is hard to believe she is the same young lady," Mrs. Harris added.

"Yes, she is quite attractive this evening. Almost too much so. The men seem to flock around her," Mr. Fairchild said disgruntledly.

Their conversation died as the music ended, and the many couples left the dance floor.

Emma approached them on Mr. Westcott's arm and prepared herself for Mr. Fairchild's displeasure. But she would not turn her back on Mr. Westcott just to please some outrageous desire of Richard Fairchild!

"Emma, I am delighted to see you at last," Mr. Fairchild said, taking her arm possessively before giving a cool nod to her escort. "Westcott."

"Good evening, Mr. Fairchild. Miss Chadwell, I will return later for our dance."

Emma could have wished Mr. Westcott had not felt it necessary to inform Richard he had signed her card for another dance, but it was too late. The man excused himself, leaving Emma to face the angry scowl on Richard's face.

"Do you have any dances for me?"

"Yes, I told everyone you had requested the last two dances, since I did not know exactly when you would be arriving," Emma said coolly, refusing to be intimidated by his anger.

Before Mr. Fairchild could express his appreciation for such consideration, if that was his intent, they were interrupted by Emma's next partner, and he watched in frustration as she took her place in the formation for the country dance. He was consoled only by the fact that her partner was a young puppy guaranteed to be harmless.

Emma avoided Richard whenever possible, since his face still held promise of a stern lecture. She would not refuse Mr. Westcott. He was a friend, sort of. Besides, she and Richard were not yet married. There was no reason for him to object to her dancing with others.

When she finished the dance before Mr. Westcott's, Emma was escorted to Mrs. Fairchild by her partner. Richard had been distracted by an old friend, and she breathed a sigh of relief. She exchanged a conspiratorial smile with Mrs. Fairchild, who agreed with Emma in this matter. They were both taken aback, however, when the musicians paused so the violinist could replace a string that had broken.

"Oh, drat!" Emma exclaimed under her breath.

"Perhaps a stroll about the room is called for," Mrs. Fairchild suggested *sotto voce*.

Emma gratefully agreed, and had just risen to accompany her when her arm was caught by Mr. Fairchild.

"Going somewhere, my dear Emma?"

She turned to stare wide-eyed at her fiancé. "Why, yes, I was going to accompany your mother on a stroll about the room."

"I think not. Mother, Emma is going to spend the next few minutes with me."

"I do not wish—"

"I know," Mr. Fairchild assured his protesting companion. "You have made that abundantly clear, my dear, but you and I have several things to discuss. We will return in a moment, Mother."

Mrs. Fairchild cast a sympathetic smile at Emma and shrugged her shoulders.

There was nothing for it. Emma stopped protesting and docilely accompanied the tall man through the crowd. She would not make a scene here.

He led her to the library and closed the door behind them. Emma looked around the room, pretending to admire the Adam fireplace, the warm fire crackling in the hearth, the numerous books, but Mr. Fairchild had no interest in his surroundings.

"I want you to avoid Mr. Westcott after this evening."

Emma stared up at his frowning face. "Why?"

"Why? Because it is causing talk. He is looking for a bride. Why is he spending time chasing after an engaged woman?"

"He has requested nothing out of the ordinary. It is acceptable to dance two dances with an acquaintance."

"This is different."

"Why?"

"Because . . . because I say so. I am to be your husband, and you must accommodate my wishes."

"How strange. I thought *you* were supposed to accommodate *my* wishes! Is that not how a courtship goes?" Emma demanded in taunting tones.

"No! That is not how a courtship goes! And what do you know of courtships! Before you became engaged to me, no one even asked you to dance!"

Emma gasped in pain, and Mr. Fairchild became even more enraged at himself than with Emma, but he could not back down now.

"You are quite right, Mr. Fairchild. You have brought me into fashion, dressed me, given me jewels. In other words, you feel you have bought and paid for me! Well, I am not for sale! Here, h-here is your ring," Emma shouted as she began tugging at the fabulous yellow diamond, hurt fueling her anger.

"Don't be ridiculous! What do you think would become of you if you were not engaged to me! Your brother would never forgive you, money-minded as he is!"

"That is not your concern, sir! I have no intention of being engaged to a dictator such as yourself, who . . . w-who cares nothing for m-my happiness," Emma protested, sobs beginning to break through her control.

"You will not break our engagement and make me the laughingstock of Society. I will not stand for it. Remain here and I will get the carriage! I am taking you home!"

When the door slammed behind him, Emma covered her face with her hands and let the tears flow. She fell to the sofa, the sobs racking her body. She could not give up Melissa, Mrs. Fairchild, Fairchild House . . . and most especially Richard Fairchild. They had become her whole life! But she could not allow him to run roughshod over her, she protested. But if it meant living without him . . . never seeing him again . . . She was surprised to feel strong arms around her and, thinking Richard had returned to apologise, she sobbed into his shoulder, "R-Richard!"

"No! No, it is Westcott, Miss Chadwell. Whatever is the matter?"

Emma lifted her head off his shoulder to stare up at the man in shock.

"Has that man hurt you? How may I serve you? You know I will do anything for you. Will you marry me, Miss Chadwell? I will do everything in my power to make you happy."

Emma stared up at the man, unable to believe the turn of events. She was even more shocked when the door swung open again to reveal Mr. Fairchild. "Oh! Oh . . . Richard!"

Mr. Fairchild had felt pangs of remorse almost from the moment he left Emma. He ordered the carriage, and then he returned to the library to make amends and take his fiancée home. To find her in the arms of another man, the very man he had suspected of trying to steal her, was too much.

Emma jumped up from the sofa. "Please, Richard! It is not what you are thinking!"

"What I am thinking, ma'am, is that I have been the worst of all fools! Why did you not just ask for your release? Was it necessary to trick me, to betray me in such a manner?" he roared. "Do not bother to return the many things my family has purchased for you! They will serve as a wedding present for you and a lesson for us! Ever the fool, I believed you were not like other women. Good evening!"

Emma stared at the slammed door as if he would come back if only she concentrated. Mr. Westcott, horrified at the turn of events but willing to accept such a gift, rose to take her in his arms. "No!" Emma protested. "No, do not . . . do not touch me!"

"But Miss Chadwell, Emma, I love you. I want to marry you!"

"No! I . . . I am engaged to Mr. Fairchild!"

"Poor child. You are in shock. Did you not hear him? He has cast you off. Accept my offer, and I will make you the happiest of all women."

Emma backed away from the man, her eyes filling with tears a second time. "I don't want to marry you. I love Richard. I will al-always love Richard!" She covered her face once more to hide the tears that coursed down her cheeks.

"But I love you. I promise I will take good care of you. It does not matter if you love him. I love you!"

"You don't even know me, Mr. Westcott. You fell in love with an image created by Richard. *He* may not love me, but he proposed marriage to me when I was at my very worst," she proclaimed tragically, ignoring her knowledge of Mr. Fairchild's motives.

Mr. Westcott appeared confused and distraught, and Emma felt sorry for him. But she could do nothing for him. She could not even do anything for herself. They were two lost souls, and neither had any hope of achieving their desires.

$== 15 ==$

MRS. HARRIS AND her daughter escorted Emma home after she emerged from the library. Both ladies were intensely curious as to why Mr. Fairchild and his mother had abandoned Emma, but no one spoke during the short carriage ride.

Emma spent her time reviewing her choices. Just as Mr. Fairchild had said, she knew there was no place for her in her family if she failed to marry money. Once it became known that Mr. Fairchild had rejected her, her life would be unbearable.

Without her brother's marriage, she might have withstood the anger and frustration of her family. But as both her brother and Miss Stokie had already warned, there would be no place for her when Charlie married. It was even possible Charlie would sell the estate.

Desperately unhappy, Emma could think only of escape. She could not remain to be the brunt of the *ton*'s laughter, shunned by her own family. When she reached her room, she found her maid waiting for her.

"Nancy, I must leave here this evening."

"What? What are you talking about, Miss Emma?"

Emma steadied her lower lip and then answered, "Mr. Fairchild has—has cast me aside, Nancy. And you know my family will have no interest in me now."

"What are you goin' to do, Miss Emma? I can't believe that nice Mr. Fairchild would do such a thing. Are you sure?"

"Quite sure, Nancy. He left me in no doubt."

"Wherever you're goin', I'm comin' with you," Nancy assured her mistress stoutly.

"Oh, Nancy, I can't let you do that. I don't know where I will go, or what I will do."

"I've only stayed here 'cause of you, Miss Emma. There be nothing to stay for when you're gone." The two women hugged before something occurred to Nancy.

"O' course! You can come with me!"

"What are you talking about?"

"My sister married the butler at the house where she was in service, and when her master died, he left her husband a tidy sum. Together they opened a little inn at Meckleston. They keep writin' me and tellin' me to come work for 'em. We'll both go there. You can decide what to do and will have a safe place to stay until then."

"Oh, Nancy, would they have me? That would be perfect. I'll work for my keep and—"

"You'll be doin' no such thing! You're a lady, and I'll thank you not to forget it! Now, we've a lot to do if we're to be off on the early stage."

"But, Nancy, I don't even have enough money for the tickets for the stagecoach."

"No, lovey, but I do. And we'll filch a little extra from the house funds. You know where they are since you used to take care of the bills, don't you, love?"

"Yes, but since my brother took over, I feel sure the bills have not been paid and the cupboard is bare. But I will check and see. Have he and Mama returned?"

"Not yet."

"Then I'll go down now, before they arrive. You come keep a lookout, Nancy. I don't want to be seen."

The two hurried down the stairs, and Nancy took up a position in the hallway, chatting with the butler who awaited the arrival of his master and mistress, while Emma found the cash box used for the household accounts. By some strange luck, her brother had left several pound notes in the box, and Emma took them without hesitation. After all, she had worked long and hard on the estates without any recompense.

Just as she emerged from the room, a carriage was heard drawing to a halt. With a quick look at Nancy, both women hurried up the stairs to lock themselves in her room.

The rest of the night was spent packing. Emma refused to pack the new gowns provided her by Mrs. Fairchild, though she hated the thought of donning once again the horrors her stepmother had chosen. With a last tearful look at the pearl necklace she'd never worn, she wrapped it and her beloved ring, along with the topazes, in a package.

Included was a letter to Mrs. Fairchild. The writing was shaky and the ink blurred by tears, but she did not rewrite it. Time was too precious.

As the sun crept up over the roofs of London, the two women stood at the door of Emma's room, tired but determined. They had accomplished their tasks. All that remained was to make their escape.

"You have the package for Mrs. Fairchild?" Emma asked for the third time.

"Yes, lovey, I have it. I will give it to Joseph when we go downstairs. He will do as I ask."

"Yes, well . . . I guess we must set out, Nancy. You are sure you want to come with me?"

"O' course, child. Let's not be dawdling 'ere. Come along." Nancy pulled the rope that would summon one of the maids to them. When she arrived, she was startled to find both women dressed with two trunks sitting at their feet.

"Lucy, please go back downstairs and send up Joseph and William and wrap some bread and cheese in a basket, enough for several meals. And keep quiet about all this," Nancy ordered firmly while Emma stood with her back to the others, staring around the room. So much had happened since her arrival in London.

"Yes'm. What be—"

"Never you mind, child. Just help the mistress this once," Nancy said firmly.

"Oh!" Lucy wanted to ask more questions, but Nancy's stern look sent her scurrying down the stairs. In no time at all, the two women were standing in the front hall, their trunks beside them, a basket of fragrant bread and cheese under a starched white napkin on Nancy's arm. They were awaiting the hackney cab Joseph had gone to fetch.

When they heard the sounds of a carriage, Nancy pulled the heavy door open. There, coming up the steps, was the master, decidedly the worse for wear. Nancy shut the door and pulled Emma after her to the butler's pantry.

"Mr. Walters," Nancy hissed, "it's the master. What if he sees the trunks!"

By now, all the staff, other than Charles Chadwell's valet and Mrs. Chadwell's maid, had been alerted to their departure. "Do not be concerned, Nancy," Walters said, supremely indifferent to the peril. "His Nibs never notices anything when he comes in at this hour."

The two women huddled in the small room, listening to the rumble of voices fearfully. But it seemed Walters was correct. He returned to report there was no problem, though it would be best to give the master several minutes to ascend the stairs and reach his room. He was quite slow after a night on the town.

In no time at all, though it seemed forever to Emma, they were riding in a hansom cab to the Lion's Head Inn, where the stagecoaches left London for all points north. Nancy dealt with the tickets, purchasing inside seats, and they just had time to see their trunks put in the boat and enter the coach before the driver ascended to the roof of his vehicle, cracked his whip, and left the dust of London behind.

Mr. Fairchild returned home from the ball angry with everyone, including himself. He had had to fend off his mother's questions about Emma's absence, and she had been unwilling to accept any of his excuses. What's more, she would be even more upset when—*if* she discovered their engagement was off.

Slamming the door of the library behind him, a sound that warned his servants to be quick about serving him, Mr. Fairchild strode over to the brandy decanter and poured himself a stiff drink. He was not too happy about it himself, he admitted reluctantly. After his infatuation with Diana, he had promised himself he would never care for another woman, but, he admitted, he did. Emma had become very important to him.

Why? She was not beautiful! She was not even pretty. Of course, now that his mother had the dressing of her, there was a certain elegance about her. And her big brown eyes were certainly warm and loveable. And when she was happy, her smile lit up everyone around her. He remembered the way she smiled at Melissa, and how she cuddled the little girl against her. He pictured her as she had looked tonight. He had intended to tell her that her gown was too revealing, but he had to admit she looked well in it.

But that thought brought back the picture of her in Mr. Westcott's arms, and Mr. Fairchild swallowed a large dose of brandy. She would probably marry the man and move to the country, and he would never see her again! Somehow, that did not please him. It should have, he told himself sternly. After all, she had betrayed him!

He poured himself another drink. Yes, that was the ticket. Think about her betrayal. Then, perhaps, he could forget her honesty, her honour, her laughter, her love for his daughter, her . . . Bah! This was getting him nowhere! He took another drink.

It was just as well. After all, she would have expected him to stay by her side when they married. She may have said she understood his plans, but once the knot was tied, she would have changed her mind. All women did that! Look at Diana. Of course, his conscience reminded him, Emma was not Diana. She did not expect him to kowtow to her beauty, to play the eternal suitor. She hadn't expected it of him when he *was* her suitor.

It was his mother who reminded him of his duty, not Emma. She had suffered the slights of the *ton* without a word. And he remembered the day he brought her the ring. She had been reluctant to accept it, concerned about the cost. Whenever had Diana worried about such a thing?

No, Emma would not have insisted on his remaining at her side. She was not selfish, thinking only of herself. Even had they . . . even were she increasing, she would not try to hold him at her side. Richard knew that instinctively.

But the thought of Emma carrying his child brought a rush of tenderness that surprised him. He would not leave her even if she urged him to, he knew.

And that was what frightened him about Emma. Even though she never asked for his heart, it was hers for the taking in spite of his intentions. He had fallen in love with Emma Chadwell. That called for another stiff drink.

Was he to lose all chance of happiness to that thief Westcott? Though his thoughts were becoming a little more hazy with each drink, Mr. Fairchild slammed a hand down on his desk and shouted, "No!"

The butler, hovering in the hall, raced into the room. "You called, sir?"

"No, I did not call," Mr. Fairchild snarled. But as the butler turned to go, he added, "Call me at ten in the morning, Perkins."

"Yes, sir. Shall I call Mr. Jenkins to help you to bed now, sir?"

"No! I . . . I am not yet ready for bed."

"Yes, sir," the butler agreed dubiously, and closed the door.

Damn! What was he going to do about Westcott? He could challenge him to a duel, but those were outlawed now and he had no intention of spending the rest of his life a fugitive. Besides, he was engaged to Emma. Mr. Westcott had no right to . . . That was it! He had a legal right to Emma. He would inform Mr. Westcott of that first thing in the morning. And then he would inform Miss Emma Chadwell that she had better make up her mind to marrying him, because he would refuse to release her from her promise.

He drank several more glasses in celebration of his decision. Then it occurred to him that Emma might plead for her freedom to marry Mr. Westcott. After all, she had never promised to love him, only to marry him.

Could he withstand Emma's pleading to force her into a marriage she did not want? With a groan, he fell into a chair. Of course not. He could not do that to Emma. He could not bear to see her brown eyes stricken, tears falling, her face pale with unhappiness.

Perhaps she preferred Westcott because he was a bachelor and had never married. Emma deserved a husband who had no shadows in his past, Richard decided, his eyes tragic as he stared across the room.

Memories of Emma holding Melissa chased those particular fears away. She might prefer a bachelor, but she loved Melissa. He had no doubt about that, at least.

But he doubted that she cared about him. He took another drink to console himself. And so the night progressed, Mr. Fairchild alternately hopeful and despairing, and a drink to accompany each mood.

Dawn was breaking when he finally stumbled up the stairs to fall facedown on his bed, clothes and all, and drift off into a troubled sleep. When Perkins informed Jenkins that the master wished to be called at ten, that individual crept into the master chamber and stared at his employer. Somehow he doubted the wisdom of carrying out those orders, but he proceeded to do so.

"Wha . . . Go away!" Mr. Fairchild muttered.

"Sir, you told Mr. Perkins you wished to be called at ten."

"Changed my mind! Go away!"

Jenkins did not wait to be told twice. Mr. Fairchild was a good master, but he expected to be obeyed.

The same occurrence took place several hours later, and again Mr. Fairchild tried to dismiss his tormentor. His head was throbbing and he ached all over. This time, however, the person would not go away.

"Come now, Richard, is this any way to greet a friend?"

"James?" Mr. Fairchild muttered, barely opening one eye to verify what his ears told him.

"Of course. What's to do?"

Richard groaned and buried his head in the pillow. An insistent hand on his shoulder gave him no opportunity to retreat.

"Go away, James."

"I can't do that. I promised Deborah I would see if there was ought amiss between you and Emma."

Richard Fairchild grew still as memories from the previous night only added to his headache. Without saying anything, he pushed himself upright on the bed and turned his bleary-eyed gaze on his friend. "What makes you think—"

Lord Atherton cut in ruthlessly. "Because you and your mother left early last night without taking your leave of anyone, and Deborah and her mother saw Emma home. Though Emma said nothing, Deborah said her face was tragic."

Mr. Fairchild turned his back to Lord Atherton and buried his face in his hands. "Go away, James."

"Wouldn't it help to talk of it?"

"No, I don't think it would. I must dress and go see Emma. I think I did something very foolish last evening."

"What?"

"If my memory does not fail me, I believe I begged off our engagement."

"What? How could you do such a thing? To Emma? She cares for you!"

"Ha! If she cares for me, why was she in the arms of another man!"

"Emma? You cannot mean it! I will not believe it of Emma. Why, she is as honest as a man of honour can be!"

"I know that!" Mr. Fairchild grated. "But I still saw her in Mr. Westcott's arms!"

"Did you ask her to explain?"

"No," Richard said morosely. "I lost my temper."

More gently, Lord Atherton asked, "And have you asked yourself why you lost your temper?"

"She is engaged to me. She has no right to be in another man's arms!"

"Richard—"

"All right, all right! Yes, I know why I became so enraged. I care for her, in spite of swearing I would never do so again!"

"But she is not like your first wife."

"I know," Mr. Fairchild agreed wearily, "but it may be too late for my sudden wealth of knowledge. I don't know if she will forgive me. She may be in love with Westcott."

"Nonsense. She cares for you, man!"

"Do you think so?" Mr. Fairchild asked incredulously.

"Deborah does, and I would trust her judgement. For a young lady, she is very wise," Lord Atherton said with pride.

"But I may have given her a disgust of me. I did not behave well last night. What should I do?"

"Why, go see her, Richard. Get down on your knees and plead with her to forgive you."

"I suppose so. What if she refuses to see me?"

"Richard, where is that domineering, forceful man who insisted on offering matrimony to her in the midst of a crowd?"

"Yes, of course. You are right. I'll just . . . ," he began as he stood, only to fall back to the bed with a groan. "Oh! I must have drunk an entire bottle of brandy last evening."

"You'll just have to suffer. I will accompany you to the Chadwells'. I don't dare return to Deborah until I can reassure her about the two of you."

Within the hour, the pair trod up the steps to the Chadwell town house. Walters opened the door and allowed the two men to enter.

"We've come to see Miss Chadwell," Lord Atherton announced, while Mr. Fairchild stood silent and pale.

"Please be seated," Walters said, gesturing to the parlour. "I'll inform Miss Chadwell you are here."

Walters pulled the door to the parlour to. Then he turned and descended to the kitchen. "Miss Smith, please inform your mistress that Miss Chadwell has two gentlemen callers."

The woman scurried upstairs. Lucy approached the august butler. "What you gonna do 'bout the young miss?" she asked in a whisper.

"I shall send you to her room to inform her of her guests' arrival. When you come down and inform me she is not in her room, I will then inform the mistress that Miss Chadwell seems to have gone out." With a wink to the young girl, he turned and ascended the narrow stairs.

"What do you make of it?" Lord Atherton asked his companion when the two left the Chadwells after a half-hour call. They had seen only Mrs. Chadwell, and their ears were still ringing with her praises of her son and daughter, but little of her stepdaughter.

"I will not pretend that I am not worried, James. Why would she go out without informing someone of her destination? And why today, of all days?"

"You surely don't think she has run away?"

"I don't know. Perhaps she has eloped with Westcott." Mr. Fairchild's brow furrowed in thought. "Let's go see my mother," he said suddenly. "I swear if Emma has run away, she will have gone to my mother."

"Of course! Why did we not think of that at once. She is sure to know."

Mr. Fairchild's mood lightened considerably at Lord Atherton's concurrence with his logic. He had felt decidedly uneasy the entire visit at Emma's home. But her stepmother did not even appear to know of their argument the previous evening, much less any occurrence this morning that might indicate a problem. Still, he would not feel at ease until he talked to Emma.

"Does your mother know . . . that is, did you tell her you and Emma were cross last evening?"

"No," said Mr. Fairchild, whose neckcloth seemed tight all of a sudden. "I fobbed her off with some lame excuses that I do not think she believed."

"No, mothers never do. It always amazes me how they see right through our schemes and lies."

"Please, James, do not be philosophical this morning. I have too many things on my mind."

Lord Atherton smiled but remained silent. He understood his friend's concern. Had it been Deborah, he would have been beside himself with worry.

When they reached Mr. Fairchild's town house, he asked the butler, "Has my mother descended yet this morning?"

"She asked for a tray in her room, sir," the man said with a bow.

"Ah, would you tell her I need a few words with her if she would not mind joining me in the library." The butler turned to follow his directions, but he stopped him. "Oh . . . has my mother had any visitors this morning?"

"No, sir."

With a nod to send the butler on his way, Mr. Fairchild led his guest to the library, pausing only to ask a footman to send to the kitchen for a pot of tea.

"We might prefer something more potent, but my mother loves tea, and I want to turn her up sweet."

At first, the men made idle conversation. Then, when half an hour had passed, Mr. Fairchild began to pace the room, his responses to his friend becoming shorter and shorter.

"What can be taking her so long?" he said. "Surely she will be down soon."

"Takes women a long time to greet the day. Might as well realise that if you are going to marry."

"Look who is talking, James. I've watched you spend as long as an hour just tying your cravat."

"Not true!" At a scornful look from his friend, Lord Atherton admitted, "Well, only when I am learning a new way to tie it."

Mr. Fairchild's response was forgotten when the library door slid open and Mrs. Fairchild entered the room. She ignored her son, but greeted Lord Atherton pleasantly if rather grimly.

"Are you feeling quite well, Mrs. Fairchild?" Lord Atherton asked.

"No, my lord. I am not feeling well."

"What is wrong, Mother?" Mr. Fairchild asked, putting aside his worries to tend to his mother's needs.

The woman turned her head slowly and stared at her son. "I do not believe you need ask, sir."

Mr. Fairchild, an intelligent man, realised at once his mother knew at least of his fight with Emma the night before, if nothing more.

"Have you heard from her, Mother?"

Mrs. Fairchild turned and stared out the window before nodding slowly. She had received the letter and accompanying parcel when she first arose and, after reading the pitiful note, wanted to skin her son alive. She was able to speak civilly to him, but it was an effort.

"What did she say? Where is she? Is she all right?"

With a scornful stare at her anxious son, Mrs. Fairchild said, "I do not know where she is. Nor do I know whether she is safe. Her message said you had withdrawn your offer. She sent her love to Melissa and to me, and she explained that she could no longer remain with her family."

Mr. Fairchild turned away from his mother, his eyes dazed as he took in her words.

"But did she say nothing about where she would go, ma'am?" Lord Atherton asked.

"No, my lord. She asked if I would provide a reference in regard to her ability to work with children should anyone enquire, so I must assume she intends to seek employment." Mrs. Fairchild sniffed, unable to hold back tears.

Mr. Fairchild whirled around and moved to his mother, taking a resisting hand in his. "Mother, I swear I had no intention of . . . I did not intend to harm Emma."

"No! But just because she is not beautiful, not greatly admired by the *ton*, you thought she had no feelings!"

"That is not true!" Mr. Fairchild shouted, losing control at such an accusation. "I love her! But she was in the arms of Westcott! I thought she was betraying me!" He turned away, afraid he would fall apart in front of their very eyes. "I panicked. I could not face another marriage full of betrayal."

"Emma is not like Diana," Mrs. Fairchild stated, hope flickering that the damage could be repaired.

"I know that now. But it is too late. She has gone."

= 16 =

"You surely are not going to abandon her?" Mrs. Fairchild asked in disbelief.

"No, I did not mean that. It is only . . perhaps she wants to marry Mr. Westcott."

"Men!" Mrs. Fairchild exclaimed. "She cares for you, though I do not know why! Such a thickheaded—"

"Are you sure, Mother?"

"Of course I am sure."

"Then why would she run away? I called this morning to apologise for my temper and to discover her feelings, but she was not there."

"It is as she said. Her family would cause a big row should they discover they would not receive the settlement."

"But surely they would not abandon her. Why would she run away? We must find her," he added before either of the others could speak. "James, you call on Deborah and her mother to be sure Emma has not gone to them for protection. Mother, would you come with me back to Mrs. Chadwell? We will confront her with Emma's note and see if she knows aught of her daughter's disappearance. If she does not, I want to question some of the servants."

Lord Atherton left immediately, but Mrs. Fairchild stopped her son as he, too, prepared to carry out his plan. "Richard, I am sorry for my anger. I . . . Emma is such a sweet, caring child. I love her almost as much as I love you. I did not want to see her hurt."

Smiling warmly at his mother, Mr. Fairchild said, "I am glad you feel that way about Emma, Mother. If you are right and she cares for me, then I will do all in my power to make her a member of our family, and together we will cherish her forever."

With agreeing smiles, the two set out for their confrontation with Mrs. Chadwell.

Not overly interested in her stepdaughter's outing, Mrs. Chadwell was in her bedroom trying a new cure for wrinkles, a white cream that smelled of rotten eggs, its main ingredient.

When informed of her callers, she shook her head impatiently and said, "Tell them I am not at home. I have already spent a half hour with Mr. Fairchild, and I see no need to put myself out for his mother. After all, we have already snagged him."

When the butler informed the Fairchilds that Mrs. Chadwell was not at home, Mrs. Fairchild took over. "Nonsense, man, she is at home. This is a matter of some importance. I shall just step up to her bedroom if it is inconvenient for her to descend."

When Mrs. Chadwell reluctantly agreed, Mrs. Fairchild entered to discover her hostess with a paper-white painted face lying prostrate on her bed. Mrs. Fairchild drew as near as her nostrils would permit.

"Madam, I received a note from your daughter this morning informing me she was leaving the protection of her home. Can you tell me where she has gone?"

"What?" Mrs. Chadwell shrieked, sitting upright, the plaster on her face cracking in several places. "Do not be ridiculous, Mrs. Fairchild. Emma has gone shopping, that is all!"

"No, ma'am. That is not all. It seems your daughter and my son had an argument last night and . . . and their engagement was called off. My son, of course, has every intention of marrying Emma, but she has left before he can repair the damage," she added before Mrs. Chadwell fell into hysterics. "Do you have any idea where she might have gone?"

Mrs. Chadwell was breathing rapidly. "We will insist on

receiving the settlements no matter what Emma has done, Mrs. Fairchild, and you may inform your son of that. After all, it is his fault. You have already admitted as much."

"Are you an unnatural mother? I tell you your daughter has disappeared, and all of your concern is centred on money?" Mrs. Fairchild stared at the other woman as if she were a monster.

"Of course I am concerned. But Emma has always been a disappointment to me. The only thing she accomplished was attracting your son, and she has spoiled that. Why can she not be more like Aurora!"

"For the last time!" Mrs. Fairchild almost shouted. "Do you have any indication of your stepdaughter's destination?"

"Well, there is no need to get huffy, Mrs. Fairchild. She has returned to our country estate, of course. Where else would she go?"

"I do not know, but we intend to find her. When we do so, madam, you may rest assured she will not be brought back to this house, where she is unappreciated."

"You are overwrought, Mrs. Fairchild. But if you want her to visit you, I certainly have no objection. I'm quite wrapped up in planning Charlie's wedding. But you must tell her I am severely disappointed with her!"

"You may be disappointed with Emma, but I can assure you she is a delight to the Fairchilds!"

Slamming the door behind her, Mrs. Fairchild left, well satisfied with her side of the battle. Mrs. Chadwell stared huffily at the closed door, unable to think of a retaliation other than an exasperated, "Well!"

Mrs. Fairchild descended the stairs to her son waiting impatiently in the hall. "Did you talk to any of the servants?" she asked.

"Yes. Did her mother tell you anything?"

Mrs. Fairchild stared at the impassive butler before saying, "If you are finished, let us depart. I will tell you later."

Once outside on the steps, Mr. Fairchild could wait no longer. "Well?"

"The woman had no idea Emma was gone and does not

care, if you ask my opinion. Her concern is that if something has happened to Emma you might not pay the settlement!"

"Mother, you must be exaggerating."

"No! I am not! She is inhuman!"

"She had no idea where Emma could be?"

"She said she must have returned to their country estate, that she had no other place to go. Did you discover anything from the servants?"

Mr. Fairchild took his mother's arm and led her down the steps, frowning. "Hmmm, it is possible she returned to their estate, but if she said in her letter her family would not forgive her if we were not to be married, it seems difficult to believe she would go there."

"But what did the servants say?" Mrs. Fairchild asked again as her son assisted her into their carriage.

He joined her and signalled the coachman to proceed home before answering her. "The butler said nothing other than confirming what we already knew, that Emma left this morning. However, I spoke with a young maid, Lucy. She refused to say anything until I explained why I wanted to find Emma," Mr. Fairchild said. "Then she told me all she knew about Emma's disappearance."

"What did she tell you?"

"Emma left with her maid, Nancy. The maid does not think they went to the estate. She does not know their destination, but she did say that Nancy has a sister who owns an inn in Meckleston. Nancy often told her that when she left the Chadwells, she would go to her sister's."

"And you think Emma has gone to Meckleston with Nancy?"

"It sounds more likely than the other."

Mrs. Fairchild agreed with her son. "You will go there to find her?"

"As soon as I can have my greys put to my curricle."

"Shall I go with you?"

"No. She has her maid with her."

"I should tell you that I will not have her returning to that house. They do not appreciate her. Bring her straight to me. It is almost two weeks until your wedding."

"Thank you, Mother. Why do you not return to Fairchild House and I will bring Emma to you there."

"All right. I will leave in the morning. When do you think you and Emma will arrive?"

"I am not sure, but it will be several days. If she is travelling by stage, it may be possible for me to arrive before her if I leave at once and take back roads, but it is a two-day drive, even travelling swiftly."

Upon their return, Mr. Fairchild prepared for his journey. When he descended a half hour later, his mother was waiting with a large basket.

"Here are some provisions so you will not have to wait when you change the horses. May God go with you, son. Bring her safely home."

"I will, Mother, I will."

The dust stirred up by the stagecoach had settled thickly upon Emma's attire, making the blue of her dress look more like an old grey. Sighing, she pulled her cloak more tightly around her to shield her gown from the intrusive grains of dust. It had been a wearying three days. Even more tiring had been her fears about the future.

She wondered if Mrs. Fairchild had gotten her package. And her heart ached for Melissa. Had she been told her Emma would not return? Emma could only hope that the little time spent with her father while Emma was at Fairchild House would be enough to encourage Richard to love his daughter. Melissa deserved that.

"We be almost there, lovey. It won't be long now before you can rest .. and get properly cleaned," Nancy added as she brushed off the sleeve of her dress in disgust.

"Thank you, Nancy. I know you are as tired as me. Are you sure your sister won't mind us coming? After all, we have had no opportunity to warn her."

"She'll be that glad to see me, Miss Emma, she won't even think of complaining," Nancy assured her with a grin.

The stagecoach horn announcing their arrival to a stop drew everyone's attention. There was a general shifting as all the occupants looked forward to a brief respite from their travels. The horses were pulled to a halt amid shouts and servants scurrying in the yard of a quiet, unprepossessing country inn.

"Why, I'll be . . . Sister and her husband have become the stop for Meckleston. Why, she'll be full to bustin' over such an accomplishment."

"Is—is that good?"

"Miss Emma, that's wonderful. It'll be a wonder if she has a spare bed."

"Oh."

Emma could understand Nancy's pleasure in her sister's accomplishments, but she had been longing for a hot bath and a clean bed from which she did not have to arise at an ungodly hour and climb back into the swaying monster that had conveyed her halfway across England.

"Never you mind, Miss Emma. She'll find something for us," Nancy reassured her companion, as if reading her mind.

Emma smiled weakly and followed the other passengers off the coach, Nancy right behind her. They were both assisted by a middle-aged man, upright in carriage, his head covered by a reddish grey stubble and his face weathered by nature.

"William, is that you?" Nancy cried as he assisted her to the ground.

The man answered slowly, his eyes searching her face, "Aye . . . I'm William, but . . . Nancy? It be Nancy?" he demanded suddenly, excitement raising his pitch.

"Certainly. And who else would it be?" Emma's maid demanded gaily. "Where is Jane?"

Nancy was wrapped in a bear hug before there was any answer, but the man eventually said, "In the kitchen, cooking the meal to be served to the travellers. 'Ave you come to stay, love? Jane will be so 'appy to 'ave you!"

"Yes, I have, but . . . well, Miss Emma, let me introduce you to my brother-in-law, William Hicks. William, this is my mistress, Miss Chadwell."

The man greeted her politely, but Emma could read the confusion and questions that filled his eyes. She looked at

Nancy, but she said only, "Later, Miss Emma. Let's go see Jane now."

"Of course, Nancy."

The trio followed the other travellers into the modest inn, but where the others turned right into the common room, William led the two women to the left, through a large door that led into the rooms in which he and his wife lived.

"I'll go fetch Jane."

"Not if she's busy, mind, William. I won't be causin' you and Jane any trouble."

"Nay, Nancy, she'd skin me alive if I didn't tell her at once her sister had come."

"Nancy, are you sure—" Emma began, only to be hushed by her maid.

"Don't you worry, Miss Emma. Everythin' will be fine." Nancy took one of Emma's hands in hers, and the two sat in silence waiting for Jane's arrival.

When the door that led into the kitchen opened, Nancy rose and met her sister halfway across the room in a big hug, both women proclaiming their happiness. Emma watched, happy for Nancy but feeling odd woman out. She wondered if it had been wise for her to burden Nancy with her presence.

"Miss Emma, this is my sister Jane," Nancy said happily.

"How do you do, Mrs. Hicks," Emma said politely. "I hope . . . that is, Nancy said—"

"Now, Miss Emma, never you mind what—" Nancy began.

"I'm that pleased that you've come with Nancy, Miss Chadwell. Often she's written me about 'ow good y'are. Why don't you go up to your room and 'ave a nice wash, and then we'll talk."

Emma was greatly relieved, but she remembered Nancy's speculation about the rooms. "Are you sure you have enough room, Mrs. Hicks? I do not want to be any trouble and—and I can't pay for anything," she admitted shamefacedly.

"Now, Miss Chadwell, would I be askin' money from you, when you've taken care of my Nancy these many years?" The woman's kindness shone from her eyes.

"I think *she* took care of *me*, Mrs. Hicks, but I thank you for your hospitality."

"Good. Just follow me."

Mr. Fairchild sat impatiently in his private parlour at the inn. He had seen Emma get out of the stagecoach, which had relieved his anxiety that he might have guessed wrong about her destination, but he had heard nothing since. He had promised Mrs. Hicks to await word from her.

The door opened, and the buxomy mistress of the inn slipped through. "She be upstairs, Mr. Fairchild. As soon as she be ready, I will show her in here."

"But you won't tell her I'm here, will you? She might refuse to see me."

"Nay, I'll not reveal that, but you'd best be kind to 'er, or I'll not protect you from my sister."

Mr. Fairchild smiled warmly at the accommodating lady. "I promise I'll be kind, Mrs. Hicks. And thank you for your assistance."

Mr. Fairchild tried to organise the speech he intended to make Emma when she entered the room, but he found it difficult to do so. He had been thinking about it for three days now, while he drove speedily over back roads and then while he awaited the arrival of the stagecoach.

He wanted to believe that Emma cared for him, as his mother and James had sworn, but he was not sure. And he was scared to confess his own love. What if she did not care for him? It would put him at her mercy, just as his infatuation had done to Diane, his wife. She had then done everything she could to kill that love, taking advantage of his weakness at every turn.

He jumped in surprise to hear Mrs. Hicks's voice providing a warning of Emma's arrival. "This way, Miss Chadwell. I'll serve you as soon as the stagecoach has taken its leave."

"Please, Mrs. Hicks," Emma said sweetly, "I can eat in the kitchen. I do not want to be any trouble."

"It'll be no trouble, Miss Chadwell. You'll see."

Emma smiled and preceded her into the room indicated.

The landlady whispered, "God bless you, child," before shutting the door.

Emma stared over her shoulder in surprise, not understanding the woman's last words. At the sound of a chair scraping against the floor, however, she jumped and turned, thinking it was a mistake that Mrs. Hicks had placed her in a private sitting room that was already occupied. Then she saw the occupant.

"M-Mr. Fairchild! What—"

Richard Fairchild stood frozen in his tracks, though he wanted to sweep the young lady up into his arms. She looked neat and tidy, her hair braided around her head in a becoming fashion. She was his very dear Emma, and he wanted her back again.

"Miss Chadwell," he began formally, not knowing how to address her.

"What are you doing here? Are any of my family with you?" Emma asked.

"No! No, your family is not with me. They do not know where you are."

"Oh!" Emma reached for the nearest chair, her limbs suddenly weakened in relief.

"Are you all right?" Mr. Fairchild asked in alarm as he rushed to help her to a chair.

"Yes . . yes, of course. I am just tired from our journey. Are you travelling on business?"

"No. I came to find you."

"But how—"

"A little maid at your mother's home, Lucy, suspected this to be your destination, and she told me."

"You did not put her position in danger?" Emma protested.

"No, of course not! But if I did, she may come to work for us," Mr. Fairchild said steadily.

Emma turned away, unable to continue looking at him when her heart ached so.

"Emma, please, I must . . . Emma, will you forgive me for my stupid jealousy of the other night? Do you care for Mr. Westcott? Is that why you ran away? Are you hoping to marry him?"

When she turned to look at him in shock, he continued, "I called on you the next morning to discover if you would forgive me. When you were not there, what was I to think?"

Even though she loved him, Emma could not resist saying, "If I had wanted to marry Mr. Westcott, I would have done so. He proposed to me."

"What? Why, that scoundrel! You are engaged to me! He cannot do that!"

Emma smiled briefly at his rage. "He thought . . . that is, he had heard talk of the *ton* and he knew you were marrying me because of Melissa."

"What has that to do with anything?" Mr. Fairchild demanded, still outraged.

Trying to hide her disappointment that he had not denied his motive, though she had begun to hope that his presence here meant that, Emma said quietly, "He said he cared for me and he thought I would prefer that kind of marriage to the marriage of convenience you offered."

"And would you?"

Emma stood and moved away from Richard Fairchild's magnetic presence to stand by the window. "No."

"Why?"

"Because I love Melissa!" Emma said fiercely, determined to protect her feelings from his scorn.

Mr. Fairchild stared at the perplexing young woman before a cunning look came over his face. "Then perhaps it would be better if I hired you as Melissa's governess."

The hurt in her eyes before she hid them from view made him feel a cad, and he strode over to her side to grasp her shoulders. "Emma! I did not mean it. I care for you, Emma! I want you as my wife, not a servant. I admit I was hoping to force you to confess some feeling for me. But I truly did not want to hurt you."

He watched in frustration as large tears spilled from her tightly shut eyes and rolled down her cheeks. Finally, since she said nothing, he gathered her into his arms and pressed her body against his.

"Emma," he whispered, "don't cry. Please don't cry, Emma, dear. I would never want to make you cry." He pressed his lips against her temple and continued to stroke her back. "Please, Emma."

"I did not mean to cry," Emma whispered against his shoulder, a very comfortable position, she thought. "But," taking a deep breath, she continued, "I love you, you see, and—"

"What?" Mr. Fairchild roared as he held the young woman away from him so he could see her face. "What did you say?"

"I love you," Emma said again, searching his face for any sign of fellow feeling.

She found herself with no time to discover anything as he pulled her to him again and his lips covered hers in a thorough kiss. It was a great relief when he swept her into his arms and carried her to the nearest chair to sit with her upon his lap. After the kiss, she wasn't sure she could have walked even one step.

Once settled, he renewed his assault upon her lips and Emma happily assisted him. She had no idea love could be so rewarding.

"Emma! Oh, my darling Emma, I thought I had lost you! I thought God was going to pay me back for all my sins," Mr. Fairchild confessed as he smiled down into her face. "Oh, Emma, I have been so worried about you! How could you run away from me?"

"But you broke off our engagement."

"Surely you must have known I did not mean it?"

"How could I have known that?" Emma asked indignantly.

"Well, you could have at least waited to give me a chance to make reparations."

Emma's face lost its radiance, and she said quietly, "That is just what I could not do. My family needed the settlement to pay off debts. They were already disappointed that I would not force you to advance the wedding. And both my brother and Miss Stokie assured me there would be no place for me in their home."

Mr. Fairchild gathered her against him again, holding her tightly. "Dear Emma, I am sorry, my love. I did not mean to cause you any pain."

"I must share part of the blame. I did not intend to let Mr. Westcott . . . I thought it was you."

"It should've been, my love. And from now on, it will be. Mother has insisted that I bring you straight to Fairchild House. She will not allow you to return to your mother. I believe they parted enemies over your disappearance."

Emma laughed. "You will not have to persuade me, Richard. I shall be delighted to return to Fairchild House. Oh! That means I will see Melissa at once!"

"I think I may become jealous of my own child," Mr. Fairchild mused.

Emma's shocked expression brought a smile to his face, but he was even more pleased by her actions. She cupped his face in her hands and gently kissed his lips. "I love Melissa, Richard," she whispered, "just as I will love any child we might have, but you will always be my first love."

"As you are mine," Richard assured her contentedly, "and always will be." After rewarding her generosity with a kiss, he reluctantly set her from him. "Come, let's go home."